THE ENCHANTED VOYAGE

By Robert Nathan

Here is a story of Mr. Pecket, a man who built a sailboat in his backyard, very far from the water. It would never stay afloat if placed in water, for Mr. Pecket neglected to caulk it, and it had no keel. Nevertheless, inland and to the eye, it was a boat built with the blend of fantasy, irony and humaneness—that is Robert Nathan alone . . .

For only at night would his boat set sail and all the pains and worries of life would soon be forgotten, for Mr. Pecket would dream that he was a sailor.

And on one very special night Mr. Pecket did experience his "Enchanted Voyage" and only then did he discover what life is truely about.

THE VOYAGE ENCHANTED

ROBERT NATHAN

John Curley & Associates, Inc.
South Yarmouth, Ma.

Library of Congress Cataloging-in-Publication Data

Nathan, Robert, 1894–
    The enchanted voyage.

    1. Large type books.   I. Title.
[PS3527.A74E5 1989]   813′.54   88–35296
ISBN 1–55504–885–4 (lg. print)
ISBN 1–55504–886–2 (pbk. : lg. print)

035754542

Published in Large Print by arrangement with Alfred A. Knopf, Inc. for the United States, Canada, the U.K. and British Commonwealth territories.

Distributed in Great Britain, Ireland and the Commonwealth by CHIVERS BOOK SALES LIMITED, Bath BA1 3HB, England.

Printed in Great Britain

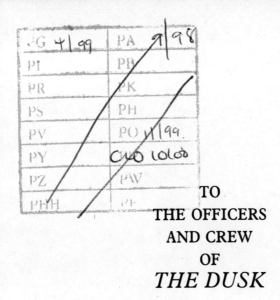

TO
**THE OFFICERS
AND CREW
OF**
THE DUSK

CONTENTS

CHAPTER I

In Which the Reader is Introduced to the Sarah Pecket, *a Small Sailing Vessel.*

Mr. Hector Pecket had a boat. He had built it himself; it stood squarely on the ground in the yard of his little home in the Bronx, very far from the water. But it would scarcely have floated anywhere else, for Mr. Pecket had neglected to caulk it, and it had no keel. Nevertheless, inland and to the eye, it was a boat; a little like an ark, but with a mast for sailing, an anchor, a windlass, belaying pins, a cabin, and a cockpit. It was named the *Sarah Pecket*, after his wife.

Mr. Pecket, who was a carpenter by trade, owned a small shop at the rear of his house. There, during the day, he built shelves for his neighbors, planed and sawed, hammered and measured, or put bits of wood together with strong-smelling glue.

But in the evening he became a ship-builder and a yachtsman. There was always something to be done on board the vessel, with a screwdriver or a chisel. At the same time he liked to imagine that he was going somewhere, that the ship was already at sea, or anchored in the Bay of Fundy.

For Mr. Pecket believed that the land was no longer a safe place on which to live. It is true, he thought, that people are more unkind than fishes who have to imagine that they are hungry before they eat each other. And he half expected a flood or some other catastrophe to put an end to humanity which was without kindness or reverence.

Uncaulked, and without a keel, the *Sarah Pecket* would have turned over in the water, and sunk. But Mr. Pecket did not worry about it; for the world seemed to him as dry as a desert. It was for this reason he had built his boat, in order to give himself, and perhaps his wife and a few others, a feeling of ocean. And every evening he allowed the *Sarah Pecket* to carry him away upon a voyage of consolation.

The currents of seven oceans, the ports of Java and Ceylon, the icy seas of Greenland, all welcomed the *Sarah Pecket*, which, however, did not leave her berth in Mr. Pecket's back yard, and did her sailing only at night, or on Sundays.

For Mr. Pecket did not wish to draw attention to himself. He realized that he was

2

not a success as a carpenter; and during the day he tried to make himself as small as possible. But at night, with the cotton sail spread above him, looking tall and strong in the darkness, he felt hopeful and safe. Blowing from the south or the east, the wind bore him from time to time a smell of the sea, and pressed against the mast with mysterious force.

At such times the *Sarah Pecket* seemed to move through the world with a swift and easy motion, carrying him away upon the tide, past the A & P grocery, the filling station, and the house of Mr. Schultz, the butcher, which rose like a little rock off his starboard quarter.

It was only in the morning, when the land was solid and real, that he felt confused and helpless. The courage which came to him at night, in the windy darkness, vanished in the daylight. Then he was no longer the captain of a ship, but a carpenter who had to make a living for himself. And each day he wondered whether he would have anything to do.

Consider him, a slight, middle-aged figure, walking down the street, carrying a pair of shelves for Mrs. Schneider's kitchen. The chances were, when he got them there, they wouldn't fit...so he carried a saw and

3

a plane along with him. And then, what was he to charge for them? When he thought how much the wood had cost, he felt ashamed to ask any more. He envied Mr. Schultz, the butcher ... meat was something everybody needed. But shelves – or a chair? They had so little value. He made his price lower and lower, until finally there was no profit in it at all.

That was the sort of thing which put Mrs. Pecket into a rage. She understood the spirit of the times; she was able to add and subtract. All right; if Mrs. Schneider wanted shelves, then she should pay for them. Or else what?

"Or else," said Mr. Pecket humbly, "she might not order them at all."

But Mrs. Pecket knew how money was made. "You're a fool," she said; and went into the bedroom and closed the door.

"You and your boat," she added, from inside.

Mr. Pecket walked down the street, carrying his shelves and his tools. He looked into the faces of men and women, and what he saw made him feel anxious and sad. It seemed to him that a new feeling had come into the world since he was young; that people no longer felt kindly disposed toward one another. Now that the bad times were

4

over, and it was possible to work again, they seemed to be looking for someone to blame for everything.

You – you have a sharp look, you dress too well. Doubtless it was you who made all the trouble in the world. Well, just keep out of my way over this.

And you, over there – you have no money and no work. To the devil with you. Perhaps you are a communist.

It was an unusually lovely autumn. The long dry spell had turned the leaves first yellow, then bronze, after which they had fallen from the trees; a sunny haze hung over everything, and the weather continued warm and still. It was weather for slow and friendly talk, hill-weather, field-weather; for roasting chestnuts, or raking leaves. Evenings came early, blue as smoke; there were no sunsets, the days faded away.

It was as if they were loath to leave, for fear of what might come later. And earth let them go with regret, as though she feared the winter, when nature also would arm herself for war, along with Italy, Germany, Austria, and Japan.

Mr. Pecket continued his way down the street in the mild October air. I would feel like singing, he thought, if it were only a question of the weather. But, as a matter of fact, I have to think about these shelves. What if I don't make enough money this winter to keep us off relief?

My wife would never forgive me.

However, that did not trouble him as much as he made believe. What caused him most concern was the knowledge that everywhere in the world people were being made to give up what they had in favor of other people who were stronger than they were. Mr. Pecket had very little to give up; but that made him all the more averse to parting with it. He had, as a matter of fact, only his liberty; but it was just this which he wished at all costs to preserve.

It seemed to him that people no longer prized it; and at the same time they did not wish anybody else to have it. Liberty, he thought: you've got to be willing to give it to others if you want to have it yourself.

A moment later, crossing the street, he gave a cry and a leap, to avoid being crushed by a taxicab which had come around the corner at full speed, and on the wrong side.

"Why don't you look where you're going?" cried the driver.

Mr. Pecket remained speechless, and trembling. The driver of the taxicab continued on his way in an angry and daring manner. He would have liked to have run over Mr. Pecket; then he would have been frightened, but, on the other hand, he would have felt less irritated.

Yes, continued Mr. Pecket to himself, just look at the dinosaurs. If you live by force, then force is what you will get. Some day that taxicab will go around a corner and bump into a truck instead of an old man with his hands full.

Mr. Pecket was not old, but after his narrow escape he felt weary, and he was glad to get to Mrs. Schneider's with his shelves. He did not expect them to fit, so he was not surprised when they turned out to be too long. Without saying anything, he sat down with his saw and began to cut. However, Mrs. Schneider was not at all satisfied with the sawdust on the floor; and when he had knocked a piece of plaster down from the wall, she felt that the time had come to say a few words.

"Now look what you've done," she said.

Mr. Pecket shook his head. "That's a queer thing," he said. "The plaster in these houses comes down easy."

"First the dirt," said Mrs. Schneider, "and now this. You've had those shelves a week; the least is, they might fit. That's how it seems to me."

"Yes, ma'am," said Mr. Pecket. "I must have got the measuring wrong."

"I suppose you think I'm going to pay for the plasterer," said Mrs. Schneider. "Well – I'm not."

"No ma'am," said Mr. Pecket. "I wouldn't expect you to. This plaster, now . . . I could put it in again."

"Not in this house, you couldn't," said Mrs. Schneider. "You've made enough mess."

Mr. Pecket returned home with the money for his shelves; but it was less than the wood had cost. He gave it to his wife without a word, and went out into the yard and sat down in the sun. I'll hear about this, he thought.

Before him stood the *Sarah Pecket,* her slender mast pointing straight into the air, the October haze settled along her decks like the breath of ocean. Mr. Pecket sat and looked at her; and he forgot his troubles, forgot the plaster which had fallen from Mrs. Schneider's wall, forgot the angry taxicab-driver. Instead, he saw the slanting shadows of the sea, and heard the sound of bells across the water; he saw in his mind the islands of the west, the line of foam, the curving beach and the hills. Nevertheless, it did not surprise him

8

when his wife followed him out into the yard.

"Well?" she said.

Mr. Pecket replied: "There was an accident. The plaster fell down."

"I can well believe it," said Mrs. Pecket. "But what did that have to do with you?"

"I suppose," said Mr. Pecket, "that while I was putting in a nail...or at least... however, there I was."

Mrs. Pecket replied: "Plaster always falls, in those cheap houses. However, I suppose you're in business for your health, so who am I to say anything?"

"I can't fight with people no better off than I am," declared Mr. Pecket.

"No," said his wife bitterly, "nor with the rich either, they scare the daylights out of you."

And pointing a finger at the *Sarah Pecket,* the woman for whom the vessel had been named, exclaimed:

"That's what's making you the laughing-stock of the whole city."

Mr. Pecket knew that the city had not yet become aware of the *Sarah Pecket;* but he felt depressed. Gone was the evening with its sound of bells, the curving beach.... He knew only too well what his wife wanted him to do, and he was determined to oppose it with his last breath. "Well," he said uncertainly, "some day you'll see."

"Yes," replied Mrs. Pecket, "I'll see. I'll see myself in the gutter, and my furniture on the street. I'll enjoy that. Or perhaps you'll take me sailing with you. I've got friends in Colorado."

So saying, she went indoors again. Left to himself, Mr. Pecket sighed, and looked up at the sky, in which the sun shone with a watery light.

"You'll see," he said again; but in a low voice, and without conviction. He wasn't quite sure what was going to happen. Maybe there'd be a flood, but it still seemed very far away.

CHAPTER II

In Which the True Sarah is Revealed, in Bed and Out.

Mrs. Pecket was a realist; she believed that life was a battle, and that the only ammunition worth talking about was dollars and cents. And she had thought of a way for Mr. Pecket to make some money. She wanted him to sell the *Sarah Pecket* to Mr. Schultz, the butcher, for use as a hamburger, coffee, and frankfurter stand.

It was this which caused Mr. Pecket so much anguish, for he felt that his wife wished to deprive him of the refuge in which he often felt noble and at peace. Mrs. Pecket, on the other hand, lived in the world as it was. "There he sits," she told her friend Mrs. Schultz, "in his private boat, while my clothes drop off in rags around me. A sailor. Ho."

And she showed Mrs. Schultz a hole in her coat.

"What use is a boat to me?" she asked.

11

Mrs. Schultz made a cluck with her tongue. "My husband is a wonder for using things," she declared. "No part of an animal is so small it can't do him any good. The livers, the lights, the brains, the bones for marrow, or soup – the tail, even – everything is used."

Placid and kind, she was happy to think that the world was so full of useful things. And she agreed with her friend Mrs. Pecket that the boat would make a good lunch-counter. "Everywhere they have restaurants that look like trains," she said, "so why not, just for once, a boat?"

But Mr. Schultz, who knew how to make use of an ox, was not sure of his ability to make a profit from the *Sarah Pecket*. When the proposition was placed before him, he looked grave, blew his nose, and reached for a toothpick. "There's an idea there," he agreed, "but I don't know. There'd be a stove to put in – that's gas; and you'd need water...it looks like it might cost a lot of money. I couldn't afford to pay much for a boat like that, Mrs. Pecket. How would I know what I'd get back from it?"

"We could go shares," said Mrs. Pecket.

Mr. Schultz looked at the ceiling in a careful way. "Well now," he said, "I don't know. Shares...you mean you'd like to put

12

up for your half of the s⸺ fixings?"

"We're putting up the boat, aren't we" said Mrs. Pecket valiantly.

"That don't hardly count," said Mr. Schultz. "Seeing you've had the pleasure of it there in your yard all this time. It don't do to ask too much of folks these days, Mrs. Pecket. Business and pleasure each in its own place, is what I say."

Having delivered himself of this opinion, Mr. Schultz concluded with the remark:

"I'll have to think about it some more."

As a matter of fact, the idea appealed to him very much; for he liked to think of himself as the owner of a boat. He would have preferred a real boat, with salt on her sides; but he consoled himself with the reflection that, without a keel, the *Sarah Pecket* couldn't get away from him, once he'd made up his mind to have her.

He was a careful man, very tidy with money, which he treated as he did his meats, by making use of everything. And he felt at home and comfortable in the world; for his position brought him face to face with his neighbors when they were thinking about dinner. Seeing mankind at its most hopeful, in this way, he did not expect anything very bad to happen; but, at the same time, he did

13

w too great an optimism to make him ...less.

He saw the world at table; he did not wish to think about people who had nothing to eat. But Mr. Pecket saw the world from another angle; he saw it with T-square, ruler, and divider, and knew that if something is out of balance, it will fall over. When that occurred, he wanted to be on the *Sarah Pecket*, out of harm's way.

So when Mrs. Pecket told him that she wanted to sell the boat to Mr. Schultz he said No.

"I'd a lot liefer you didn't talk about it," he said, "it only gets me riled."

However, Mrs. Pecket was not afraid of riling him. "There's a chance for you there," she said, "if you only had the eyes to see it. I hate a man to be stubborn. What are you now? Just a joke, up and down the block. Sell the boat to Schultz, and you're part owner in something that's respectable and has got a profit in it. I figure it would bring you in twenty dollars a week, clear."

"You might as well ask me to sell the breath right out of my mouth," declared Mr. Pecket.

"Let's not get personal," said his wife. "Here I am telling you how to put money in your pocket; and you talk like I was

14

killing you. What's your mouth got to do with it?"

"I breathe through it," said Mr. Pecket simply.

"It's not proved you breathe at all, if you ask me," said his wife bitterly. "But you eat, I notice; though who's to pay for it, I never know."

"You haven't starved yet," said Mr. Pecket.

"Nor want to," she answered. "I'm thinking of the future."

"So am I," said Mr. Pecket, "and it says don't sell my boat."

"Not to me, it doesn't," said Mrs. Pecket. And she gave her husband a long, thoughtful look, which caused him to feel anxious.

"Don't try to do anything behind my back," he exclaimed, "because I don't care for it."

Mrs. Pecket made no reply. For the rest of the day she remained silent and mysterious and went about her housework with an air of reserve.

That night Mr. Pecket lay in his wooden bed beside his wife, and listened to the sounds of the city. Low, restless, and unending, they sounded to him like the booming of surf on the shore, like the hoarse whisper of the sea. The lisp of leather shoes

15

on the pavement, the whine of trucks, the grumble of the distant elevated, horns, cries, whistles, all blended and changed, drifted across his drowsing thoughts, turned into brine and mist, into the suck and hiss of foam rising and falling. It seemed to him that he was moving serenely across the waves; warm and comfortable, he felt around him the infinite spaces of ocean. But all at once his breath caught in his throat, and he grew moist with fright. It had occurred to him that some day he would die, and leave behind him this world, which was full of such exquisite sights and sounds.

Mr. Pecket often thought that he did not wish to die, that he wished to live. There were so many places to be seen, so many things to do.... However, when he thought that he had never actually gone anywhere or seen anything, he felt uncomfortable and ashamed; and he tried to apologize for himself. I'm not very strong, he thought, and I haven't any money. And besides, my wife would never let me leave her. But in his heart he knew that he was afraid of a world in which there was so little friendliness and love.

At the same time, he was terrified because he thought that he would die some day without ever having been truly happy.

Lying there in the dark, he thought about his wife. She will have to die too, he said to himself, and she has had no more happiness than I. He wondered if she was frightened; and he felt sorry for her. Her hair is getting thin, he thought, like mine. It comforted him that Mrs. Pecket also was mortal. The long dissolving of his flesh in the cold earth, the never-coming-up to light, the never-reaching-back to warmth, seemed less dreadful to him when he realized that it was not meant for him alone – that everyone he knew and spoke to must go with him sooner or later into the darkness, everyone – all the voices, harsh and sweet, be silent, the brown, the blue eyes give back no glance, the hands lie still without moving.

Poor Sarah, he thought, she won't like that very much, she has so many plans.

He was mistaken. Mrs. Pecket's plans saved her from the thoughts which caused her husband to shiver in his bed. She had no longings, except for what she could buy; she no longer cared to think about youth and beauty, she thought only of the struggle to live, and to get the better of the people around her. And planning for that success, busy with life and the living, she was as happy as she could be, without, at the same time, feeling any less vexed at her husband.

17

Outside her window, in the darkness, the city whispered and grumbled; its voice, made up of many voices, like the sound of bees in summer, stirred and excited her. And in the silence of her little room – a silence made sharper by Mr. Pecket's wakeful and miserable thoughts – she imagined that she was holding a conversation with her friend Mrs. Schultz. "What about the boat," she said to her; "will your husband buy it?"

"Well," said Mrs. Schultz, "he's thinking about it."

"You tell him from me," said Mrs. Pecket to the darkness, "that if he wants it, he can have it."

She settled herself more warmly in her bed. "What'll we call it?" she said.

"What'll we call what?" asked Mrs. Schultz unexpectedly.

"The boat," said Mrs. Pecket. "That's what we're talking about."

"But he won't sell it, will he?" replied her friend. "So why do we talk about it?"

"Never you mind that," said Mrs. Pecket. "I've got my own ideas. Give me a name for it. Something nice."

"Well," said Mrs. Schultz, "there's the *Old Chop House;* I always like that, myself."

"Yes," agreed Mrs. Pecket, "that's a good

18

name. It's refined. But it doesn't sound much like a boat."

And drowsily she thought of names which would sound both like a boat and a ham-burger stand. The *Half Moon*...the *American Clipper*...

"Do you want to know what I'm going to do?" she asked Mrs. Schultz. "I'm going to put wheels under it, and move it right over into your yard. Then you'll have it. Once it's gone," she said, "it's gone."

And she added in a meaning way,

"Gone and paid for."

"That's stealing, Sarah," said Mrs. Schultz doubtfully.

"Not when you've paid for it, it isn't," said Mrs. Pecket.

Presently Mrs. Schultz remarked in a small voice: "Won't he be mad when he finds what you've done?"

"Leave that to me," said Mrs. Pecket. Turning her back on Mr. Pecket, and on the ghost of Mrs. Schultz, she closed her eyes, while the corners of her mouth turned up in a smile, a little grim, but not without a certain charm.

CHAPTER III

A Waitress Leads a Lonely Life.

Mary Kelly was a waitress at the Hollywood Restaurant, on Fordham Road. Dressed in black, with an orange apron, she hurried to and fro among the tables, putting down in front of the patrons heavy dishes of cereal, ham and eggs, coffee, baked apples, and pancakes. She was agreeable and well-formed, but thin; she got her meals for nothing, but she no longer had any desire for food. There was no doubt about it, watching other people eat had taken away her appetite.

She lived in a boarding house about a mile from the restaurant, walking to her work in good weather, or going by trolley in the rain. She saw little of the city – morning light, and evening light; or sometimes, on Sunday, the zoo. However, she knew a great deal about life; for when she had a day off, she went to the movies, and there she learned how to live. It was a lesson which never failed to enchant

20

her, for she realized that what she saw was the truth. Life was like that: because it was impossible to make such things up. Seated in the dark, to the accompaniment of music, she saw poverty like her own, without, however, being the least afraid that it would fail to turn out all right in the end. She wanted, for herself, only what she saw on the screen: love, a boudoir done in silver and glass, long eyelashes and an ermine coat. She did not think it too much to expect; but sometimes she wondered if she was not in the wrong business, or the wrong part of the country for it.

The truth is, she was lonely; she had no friends, except on the screen. For she was strict, and shy. When she thought about the other waitresses, who were not above going out now and then with one of their regular customers – a salesman from downtown, or a clerk from one of the shops – she shook her head. "I wouldn't want to do a thing like that," she said to the red-headed girl at the next table, "because I'm waiting for Mr. Right to come along."

The red-head opened her eyes wide. She was unable to speak; but some time later she suddenly exclaimed: "My foot."

Mary wanted Mr. Right to find her pure, and without anything to regret. For she

21

realized that, in the end, the past always rose up, and took time to explain. And in one case, she remembered, it couldn't be explained at all. Mr. Leslie Howard was in it; and the girl had lost him. What a dreadful loss, and all because she hadn't kept herself pure. She took to drugs, and died. Still, it had all happened in London.

"Just the same," she said to the elderly lady whom she was serving with a chicken patty, "a girl has got to keep her ideals" – a statement which caused the elderly lady to gaze at the patty in astonishment, and to remark in a doubtful voice: "I suppose they do."

When she thought about the man she expected to marry, she imagined him to be a man of the world, but young and tender. She would have liked him to be a poet... but she did not know what a poet was. On the other hand, she knew – from the motion pictures – what it meant to be a district attorney, or the owner of a night club. Or, perhaps, the son of a wealthy farmer; it was nice to have a father, but they made trouble on account of not understanding the ideals of a girl like herself.

She believed that a young woman should be tender, and that her place was in the home. When she read in the morning paper about Miss Jacobs, the tennis player, or Miss Whittlesey, the sailing champion, she shook her head. That was not, she thought, the best life for a woman. For herself, she would hardly care to be a sailor, and wear clothes made of canvas, or a bathing-suit. Janet Gaynor, she thought, had a more elegant life; and one that was full of opportunities for betterment. Sailing a boat couldn't lead to anything very good, so far as she could see; it was healthy, but it lacked advancement.

And what she wanted was to advance herself in the world. She believed in goodness; and she believed that it would be rewarded.

Nevertheless, she suffered from loneliness, and depression of the spirit; and as the long autumn evenings came down, she found it harder and harder, looking out through the plate-glass windows of the restaurant at the darkening street, to think with much joy or hope of the little room she lived in, with its bed, dresser, and chair, and the solitary light hanging from the ceiling. She was never in a hurry to get there; for once shut within those age-soiled, paper-faded walls, she knew that life could never find her, that it would hurry by outside without so much as knowing she was there – life, and laughter, and love, and Mr. Right, whom there was no chance whatever of meeting until tomorrow morning.

Not that she made much of her chances in the street, morning or evening; but at least she was there, if anything cared to happen. Perhaps the man she was waiting for was going home, too, as she was; perhaps he was at the wheel of his car, his hat on the back of his head, his eyes on the girls, looking to see who might like to ride (and a little later more than ride, in some dark lane?). She would never know, for she hurried by with her face turned away, and her heart beating. Other girls stood at the curb, by ones and twos, looking up and down, smiling and arch, waiting to be asked, their arms held out to danger which did not frighten them until too late. But Mary, watching them, felt indignant and ashamed; and at the same time afraid of something, but whether it was for them or for herself, she didn't know....

Yet her thoughts raced after them, perhaps to warn, perhaps to watch; like an unopened bud, she trembled for her sisters, whose leaves were already ruffled by the wind. That wasn't what she wanted, a stranger in the dark, whom anyone could have; but she was young and lonely, and winter was coming. A lover and a friend, a banker, or a district

24

attorney...he might be driving past on his way somewhere; how could she tell?

She didn't look to see, but her heart kept telling her not to hurry. There's a dress in that window you might want to look at, it told her; don't cross the street in such a rush, wait for the lights to change. Don't forget – once you're home, you're home.

She hurried along none the less, anxious and upright, lonely and correct, a slender, dream-inveigled object, her unsafe heart tugging backward like a child, but like a child being rushed home anyway, to be put to bed and told to dream about tomorrow.

In her little room everything was neat, and smelt of cold-cream and soap. She spent her evenings tidying herself, and imagining what it would be like to live in a room of glass and silver, and not to have to wash out her stockings. As it was, there was plenty to do: holes to be darned, handkerchiefs to be laundered and left to dry against the window-pane, her own hands and hair to be tended, and her face creamed for the night. By these means she preserved her appearance, and kept up her hopes. When everything was done, she turned out the light, got into bed, and said her prayers under the covers. They were simple and direct, the prayers of childhood; only there was nobody to bless at the end, except herself.

Then she fell asleep. But first she heard the city outside her window, murmuring and talking. She was not afraid of it, it did not sound unfriendly, or impatient; it was waiting for her to bring it her fresh, thin, cold-creamed face, and her hopes and ideals. In return, it would give her a banker for a husband, and an ermine coat. There was just the question of getting acquainted, that was all. Tomorrow, perhaps – or the day after....

Nevertheless, sometimes in the rain, or on foggy nights, she wondered, with a sudden catch in her breath, how far tomorrow was away, and how long the day would be in coming....

In the morning she was full of hope again. It brought her out of bed with eyes from which the sleep had vanished, wide and light with anticipation. There was still an hour in which anything could happen, before her work began. But if it was raining, her spirits fell. Then she felt weary and hopeless. Nothing ever happened in the rain, nothing could ever happen; everything was wet and miserable.

She watched the water streaming down the windows of the restaurant, and, beyond the glass, the empty street, along which people hurried with their heads down, and their noses in their collars. It was warm and dull in the restaurant, yet the thought of going out into the rain when her work was over made her shiver. There was nothing ahead, on such a day, but the packed bus or the crowded trolley, and her own little room – no one to look at, no one to look at her, no danger, even, in the rain – nothing. Just drip drip drip, everyone to himself.... "I guess I'd go crazy," she told the red-headed waitress, "if it rained all the time."

The red-head gave her a long look. "The trouble with you is," she said, "you worry."

"There's places in the world," said Mary dreamily, "where it never rains at all, hardly. And there's an island somewhere where it rains all the time. I don't know; it's queer."

"What you ought to do," said the red-head, "you ought to go south. You know – for the winter. It's different with me; I like the winter sports."

And thinking of the winter, in which she never put her nose out of doors if she could help it, the red-headed waitress gave a snort. "Sure," she said, "you ought to go south. I'd go myself, but they can't spare me from my social duties."

Mary, to whom everything was at least

likely, gazed at her friend with respect. "Perdon me," she said; "I didn't know."

"That's all right," said the waitress; "think nothing of it." She snapped her fingers in the air. "Don't be a sucker all your life," she remarked.

But it cost so much, thought Mary; and how would she go? With a gentle and joyous expression, she imagined herself in a train being noticed by everybody. She was dressed in her best; and she was reading a book. Directly in front of her was seated the banker's handsome son. She saw the way he looked at her, out of the corner of his eye.

"Thumb a ride," said the red-head; "thumb a ride. When you get to Florida, jump. You'll know it by the palms."

And she sailed off into the kitchen, to bring back a plate of waffles for a customer. Mary looked after her with a timid smile. "Thank you," she said; "I'm sure you mean it for the best."

Thumb a ride: that was what the girls did at night, going home. A man couldn't respect a girl he'd met that way. Supposing his mother asked where had they met? The trouble with people was, they didn't think of things like that until it was too late.

Still, it was warm in Florida, and dry. A girl wouldn't have to wear her winter coat, made of shoddy in the first place, and three years old, with a fur piece from which some of the fur had worn off.... She imagined herself strolling by the sea, sunburned and dainty; with eyes closed she gave herself up to her dreams. How blue the water was; but not more blue than your eyes, Miss Kelly; or may I call you Mary? He was young, and his eyes were blue too, like Gary Cooper's.... That was his mother over there, with the white hair and the tiara.

The wet and rheumy individual at the table in front of her gazed at her gloomily. "I said a ham sandwich," he remarked to the air, "and a cup of coffee. Still, if nobody cares..."

Mary opened her eyes with a start. "What did you say?" she asked.

"Nothing," said the man. "Nothing at all. Don't let me disturb you, sister. Later, perhaps. What are you doing tonight?"

She drew herself up, and gave him a look of disdain. "Never mind what I'm doing tonight," she said. "Just give me your order, mister; that's all you have to do."

Dirty old man, she thought on her way to the kitchen; what am I doing tonight? Nothing with you, anyhow.

Nothing at all. Just nothing. I'm going

home alone by myself, if you want to know. Tonight – and tomorrow night – and the night after....

CHAPTER IV

In Which Mr. Pecket Receives a Shock.

Mr. Pecket came into his house in a hurry. "Look," he said to his wife; "what have you done to the boat?"

"What boat?" asked Mrs. Pecket. "Do you mean that thing in the yard? Nothing." And she hummed a tune, to show that her heart was steady, and her mind made up.

"You've put wheels on it," said Mr. Pecket.

He was surprised; and he looked at his wife in an anxious way. "What did you want to do that for?" he asked.

"Well, I did," said Mrs. Pecket. "And if you really want to know what for, I'll tell you. The boat has been sold, Hector Pecket – sold, and paid for, cash."

Mr. Pecket sat down. He had feared it from the first; but just the same, now that it had come, he was taken by surprise. "You didn't," he said.

"I did," said Mrs. Pecket.

"But it's mine," said Mr. Pecket. "You'd no right."

"It's done now," said Mrs. Pecket; sold lock, stock, and barrel. So set your mind at rest. Here's the money; twelve dollars, minus some I kept out to pay the grocer. Take it; it's all you'll get."

Mr. Pecket digested this news in silence. Never very forceful, or with a lot to say, he seemed to shrink and to become smaller than ever. "So you put wheels on her," he said; "well..."

In the catastrophe, his mind clung to one fact: that his life as a sailor was over. Anchored to the land, unable to move backwards or forwards, the *Sarah Pecket* might have gone anywhere. But to give her wheels was to admit that she would never see the ocean. It made something out of her no boat had ought to be.

"Why did you put wheels on her, Sarah?" he asked at last. "What made you do such a thing as that?"

"To roll her over into Schultz's yard," said Mrs. Pecket, "first thing in the morning. That's why. Maybe you don't care about making a living, Hector, but I do; and I don't aim to scrimp and save and do without clothes any more, while you play you're a sailor out in the back yard. And don't talk to me about a flood, either, because I don't feel like listening to you."

And, in a firm way, she went about setting the table for supper.

Mr. Pecket said nothing; he sat for a long time looking out of the window. After a while he went upstairs, and came down again with a blanket. Then he went into the kitchen and took a bottle of milk. "What are you up to now?" asked Mrs. Pecket.

"I'm going to sleep on the ship," said Mrs. Pecket. "Or do you grudge me that, too?"

"It's all the same to me," said Mrs. Pecket. "But don't wake me up when you come in, is all I've got to say."

Mr. Pecket went out to spend his last night on the boat. He thought of all the ports he had planned to touch at before the snow fell, the strange and secret places he had been saving up for himself. Timor Sea, and Upernivik, it was now or never for them, he'd have to hurry. Yet, after he had stowed his blanket in the cabin, he sat for a long time without drawing out his charts. Something was wrong, his heart wasn't in it; he couldn't make it seem real any more. Already sold, and fitted with wagon-wheels, the *Sarah Pecket* no longer felt like a boat to him. She was a restaurant – a hamburger stand; what was he doing there, sitting in the yard in the

33

fading light, thinking about Timor Sea? He ran his hand over the planks, up and down the rigging; with what love he had put her together, with what steadfastness she had served him. But it had all been make-believe; none of it was true, they'd never been anywhere, really. Well, it was over now, all the make-believe. She was just a wagon.

He looked at the wheels; they had belonged to a cart once, the wagon-tongue stood up past the boat's counter, tied to the stern by a piece of rope. One could steer, he guessed, by holding onto it. And there was a clumsy brake up front; he supposed that would help to get her anchored in Schultz's yard, when the time came. He walked to the bow; the brake was on, he leaned down over the port rail and let it loose. Then, although he no longer believed that he was going anywhere, he hoisted sail for the last time. The evening air was cold and moist, there was rain in it; the sail hung there like a slice.... Night came down, the windows of his home glowed like a lighthouse in the darkness. He went into the cabin, and wrapped the blanket around him.

It was over, then – the little life of his own, made up out of nothing, or nearly nothing – a few planks and some old charts. After this there would be no escape, no way of leaving, even for a moment, the world of his neighbors, none of whom were seafaring men; no way of being alone again, ever...if a flood came he'd be drowned with everybody else, tossed in with other people's doings – and no way to say to God, even: Here I am, Lord, all by myself, out on the waters...look me over.

His eyes closed; and he slept. Like an admiral or a captain, he lay on his wooden bunk, with the ship's side curved over him. And the shades of the great ships of the past drew in from sea to bid him farewell. Their towering masts rocked in the clouds from which a few drops of rain had begun to fall. Fog was in their sails; gracious and lovely they lifted their misty bows to their sister, the *Sarah Pecket*, fitted out with wagon wheels; tenderly, and with regret, they flew the signals of farewell. The wind rose, and they came closer, they passed within hail, lifting their wet shoulders, tossing the spray from their bows; green water foamed along their sides, the wind sang...louder and louder it sang, the halyards hummed, the great sails eased and filled with the sound of thunder. And the waters rose, the seas stood up, driven in over the land, over the houses...nothing was left in all the world, nothing was left but ocean, heaving and

35

rolling. The *Sarah Pecket* quivered, she tugged at her moorings, she lurched a little to starboard. . . .

Mr. Pecket woke with a start, to feel his ship keel over. Thrusting his head out of the cabin, he was met with what he took to be a wave; in his sleep-befogged mind, he saw the land tossing like the sea, and thought that the flood had come. "Sarah," he cried out in terror, "where are you?" but the next moment he saw that it was only a storm of wind and rain, before which the cotton sail of the *Sarah Pecket,* round and taut as a little moon, was doing its best to pull the vessel over onto her side. Pale with fright, Mr. Pecket grasped the wagon-tongue with both hands; in a vague way, he thought to ease her. She gave a lurch, her nose swung about in a quarter circle, the wind caught her fair aft – and the *Sarah Pecket* started slowly across the yard in the direction of the street.

There is always a great deal to do when a ship leaves her moorings: the direction of the wind must be gauged, the main sheet made fast, the stays loosed and taken up, the jib sheeted down, and obstacles such as other vessels, mooring buoys or cans, lobster pots, lamp-posts, and fire hydrants avoided. Mr. Pecket attended to everything. He was in a panic; but it did not occur to him to desert the ship. He knew that once he let go the wagon-tongue, the *Sarah Pecket* would be caught by the wind, careened against the curb, and wrecked. He thought of the brake up forward; but unless he could get the sail down first, to put the brake on would only serve to topple the vessel over onto her side. And he couldn't get the sail down as long as it was full of wind. He tried to think of what a real sailor would do, of what he'd done himself the week before in a blow off the Cape of Good Hope; but there he'd been at sea, with the whole ocean to tack about in. If I come up into the wind, he thought, I can get my sail down. Only then I'll be broadside to the traffic; on a night like this I'd be run over sure as shooting. There goes a black nun; I'm making a lot of speed. Oh help me, Lord.

He was too busy to see his house go by. When he looked up at last, he was already a hundred yards down the street, and the *Sarah Pecket* was bowling along at a good four knots, throwing up sprays from the puddles.

Mr. Pecket gazed after his house, which grew smaller and smaller behind him. A lump grew in his throat; he wished his wife had been there to see him off. It was lonely in the storm, and he felt a little frightened.

37

Still he was doing the right thing...he couldn't let the boat go, not while he had his senses....

"You thought she wouldn't sail," he said, to no one in particular. "Well, look at her now. She's a sweetheart."

And with a grim and sea-bitten air, he turned his rained-on face to the road ahead, dark as the night, and wet as the sea.

CHAPTER V

And Mary Kelly a Torn Coat.

Things had been going badly with Mary Kelly. She was lonely, but she was used to it; she was poor; she was used to that, too, but tired. She would have liked to forget for a while the struggle between what she hoped and what she got; but the little things wouldn't let her alone. That very morning there'd been no hot water in the bathroom. And at noon she'd broken a plate; that was twenty-five cents from her wages. Now it was raining. What a storm. She looked out at it in despair.

But worst of all, there was a tear in her winter coat.

When she had gone to put it on at the end of the day, she had found it on the floor, with a long rip in it. Someone had thrown it there...heaven alone knew who, or why. It must have caught in something sharp on the way down. Well, there it was.

She called it her winter coat, though as a

39

matter of fact it was simply her coat; she had no other. Made of a combination of materials known as shoddy, it did not so much keep her warm as give her the appearance of warmth. That was something, at least, if only an illusion. Now there was a jagged tear in the front of it; and even the illusion was gone.

Mary Kelly was not a realist, although that is the way she liked to think of herself. As a matter of fact, she lived in a world no more solid than a bog. It was made up of her hopes and her ignorance; and it was a world in which everything looked firm and bright. She left each tussock of illusion as it sank beneath her, only to hop happily over to the next. Thus she kept going, without ever losing her courage. Nevertheless, to lose her coat was a serious matter. If she couldn't even look warm, how could she look?

She dressed for the street slowly, and with a heavy heart. Outside it was pouring, she could hear the rain striking the asphalt, cascading down the windows. Her arms and legs felt weary from the long day's work, her whole body ached. The buses would be crowded, and long before one came along, she'd be drenched. If only she could stay where she was.... What was there outside, but water?

She thought: I'll never meet anybody now, with my coat all tore.

"Well," she said to the red-headed girl, "goodnight, I guess." And she showed her the tear in her coat. "Look," she said, "what somebody did to me."

The red-headed girl looked at it gravely. "It's a lulu," she agreed. And she added not unkindly:

"The world is full of punks."

"I guess it is," said Mary; and went out into the rain.

As the wet wind hit her, she cowered; she bent like a tree, and then, like a tree, stood up again. There was life in the wind; storming in over the city, it smelled of country, of dying leaves and wet earth – where did it come from? It was a rowdy wind, it had no patience with people like Mary. And all at once she, too, felt stormy; and, from being weary, found herself suddenly reckless, and inclined to be angry.

She'd been so careful; and what had it got her? The world was full of punks, and somebody had torn her coat. Well, he'd torn more than her coat, if he wanted to know. And now the wind . . . it handled her this way and that, it blew her about as though her feet weren't her own. All right – let her be handled; she didn't care any more.

41

It was a storm of the heart, a sudden gale of the spirit. Take the other girls, now. They rode home in automobiles; they thumbed themselves a ride. Or maybe they just looked willing, and the men stopped. It was as easy as that: just a smile, and a hop; hello, mister.

She looked up and down the street. There was a big car coming...well, Mary, what about it?

And with her heart in her mouth, she jerked her thumb in the direction she wanted to go.

The car sped by, splashing her a little as she stood at the curb. "All right," she said, "don't, then." But she was surprised; and her face took on a grim and obstinate expression.

"Going my way, mister?"

However, when three more cars had gone by without stopping, she began to think that something was wrong. I'm holding back, she thought; I don't make it interesting enough.

And with an engaging air, she stepped off the curb into the path of the fourth car, which was approaching in a cautious manner.

The driver of this car already had two young ladies with him. He was not unwilling to take a third; but he liked modesty in women; he wanted them to be willing, rather than eager. Now he swerved the car in such a way as to pass within a foot of Mary, who was full of hope, and ready to get in. But no one asked her to; instead, the young lady nearest the window thrust out her hand and gave her a sharp push. "Fresh!" she said in an angry voice, as the car went by.

Mary sat down hard in the middle of the road. She was surprised; and after a while, she realized that she was sitting in a cold puddle. It was this more than anything else which kept her from rising, for she imagined what her bottom would be like when she got up. Torn in front, and wet behind... and the world so unfriendly... she was ready to weep, from vexaton and from a feeling of discomfort.

It was at this moment that Mr. Pecket, bowling down the avenue at a good four knots, saw her sitting in the street. He had fastened his main sheet, and he had time to look about him. Well, he thought, there's a man overboard.

And without a moment's hesitation he swung the bow of the *Sarah Pecket* up into the wind.

It was a difficult maneuver, and one which might well have frightened a more seasoned sailor. However, Mr. Pecket's inexperience was a great help to him; unaware of the difficulties involved, he approached them without fear; and although he almost capsized, by that time it was too late to change his mind. The *Sarah Pecket* teetered, righted herself, and came slowly up into the wind, past Mary, who sat there like a little buoy, or a black nun. "Can I help you, ma'am?" asked Mr. Pecket.

She was a little uncertain just what it was had stopped for her – some sort of truck, she thought. "Well," she said, "if you're going my way . . ."

He helped her in over the side. Then grasping the rope tiller, and hauling in on the sail, he brought the ship off the wind again, made a creaking circle in the street, jibed her over, and started away once more, down the avenue. "My," he said, "how nice she sails."

It was then that Mary noticed what a strange truck had picked her up. "There," she said, "it's a boat."

And she looked at the mast and the sail with a startled expression.

Mr. Pecket smiled down at her. "Thank you, ma'am," he said. "That's right – it's a boat. And headed," he added as though it had just occurred to him, "for the Caribbean Sea, by God."

The oath was accidental, the result of

excitement and surprise. He had no sooner said it than he wished to apologize. But the effect on Miss Kelly was not at all what he expected. To her way of thinking, it made a sailor of him; and she murmured in a breathless voice, "The Caribbean – that's a long way off." And she gazed dreamily out ahead, into the rain.

"It is, ma'am," said Mr. Pecket stoutly; "it is, indeed. But we'll make it, if the wind holds." He squinted aloft, and felt of the starboard stay; it was tight as a string, and sang in his hand. "Hm," he said; "well...if the mast don't go over.

"But I'll drop you anywheres you say, along the road."

For a while Mary said nothing. She was thinking of the Caribbean, and of her own little empty room waiting for her – she was thinking of the long winter, of the cold and the rain and the snow, the getting up in the morning and the going to bed at night...washing out her stockings, drying her handkerchiefs against the window-pane...the endless loneliness...she was thinking of her wet behind and her torn coat....

"All right, mister," she said at last; "you can let me off in Florida."

CHAPTER VI

The World Being What it is, Mary Sets Her Course Accordingly.

They didn't have very much money, but then, they didn't need very much. Mary had her week's wages, and some left over from the week before; and Mr. Pecket had almost fifteen dollars. There was milk and bread on board, enough for a meal or two; and water along the way for the asking. He could lay in some cans of soup at the grocer's, and buy a cheap alcohol stove for cooking. The wind, at any rate, would cost them nothing; the wind was free. Full and free all the way across the city; too free, perhaps – it almost wrecked them on the bridge, sweeping down the river from the north, and howling dismally over their heads. He had to luff sail, not to be taken clean overboard and dumped into the water below. But with the sheet eased, the *Sarah Pecket* stood up to it, and made ten knots on her beam end, down the slope to Jersey.

There was a little trouble at the other side: faced with a boat where no boat ought to be, the police were of two minds about letting it go through. But Mr. Pecket had paid his toll and was off and away before anyone could think of a reason to stop him. "That was a close call," he said to Mary; "you see, we've got no running lights."

However, Mary was still sailing in her mind across the bridge, careening through space high above the water, darkness about her, and the wind singing in the sail. "My," she said, "that was elegant. Weren't we over on our side, though! I was scared all the time."

"No call to scare, ma'am," said Mr. Pecket gallantly. "I've been through worse than that." And he started to tell her about a blow he'd been in, off the Cape of Good Hope. "The waves were mountain high," he said; "I just kept her heading into them." But after a while he grew silent and confused, for he realized that this voyage was a real one, and that he would have to sail it out. A host of doubts assailed him; his heart beat, and he felt frightened. "Yes, ma'am," he muttered, "this is an awful night."

But when he looked at Mary, he felt better again. She didn't seem to be afraid. "You

47

must have done a lot of sailing, mister," she said.

Mr. Pecket took a deep breath; that made it all right again. He had needed someone to remind him, just then, of all he'd done – or at least of all he'd meant to do...someone to remind him of the man he'd always been, inside his own head. He turned to smile at Mary, to thank her for her comfort – only to see that she was shivering, wet through, and cold. "Look here," he said, "you'd best go below. I can manage all right myself. You'll find some bread and milk and a blanket down there; wrap yourself up warm. This wind'll blow us half to China before morning."

And once more firm, and with a resolute expression, he settled himself at the helm.

Mary went below; she took off her wet things, and wrapped herself up in the blanket. It was like the cabin of a ship, she thought; there was a narrow table in the middle, a shelf with two or three books on it, two wooden bunks, and an oil lantern hanging from a hook in the ceiling. She laid herself down on one of the bunks and watched it; it swung to and fro like a lantern at sea.

That's where she was, she thought – in a ship at sea. She could hear it creaking under

48

her, and the sound of wind in the rigging, it lulled her, she felt the warmth of the blanket spreading out in little circles from between her shoulder blades. Overhead, on the rainswept deck, the steersman grasped his helm; in the tiny porthole above the bunk, she could see flashes of light, like lighthouses going by. What an odd little man he was, but brave and kindly; hardly Mr. Right, she thought, but you never knew.

And she was going south, herself – to Florida, or to the Caribbean, wherever that was...to China, maybe, only that was further west. Being in a ship made it different, people went sailing together without there being anything wrong. It wasn't like being picked up by an automobile; only poor people did that. Not that this was like rich people, exactly, but still...Look how the lantern swung, backwards and forwards, backwards and forwards, almost enough to make a body seasick.... It was warm in the blanket, and peaceful; she felt very drowsy. She could hear the wind and the rain outside, but she was quite, quite safe; the ship was sailing steadily on through the night, and in the morning she'd be in Florida....

She closed her eyes. "Good-by," she said

to the red-headed waitress, "I'm off to China."

China... China...

Don't drop the tray....

But in the morning they were still in the north. She came on deck at the first light, in a startled way, rubbing her elbows and looking about her. Palm trees would not have surprised her half as much as what she saw, which was simply a brown field stretching away to a fringe of woods; and, directly in front of her, a gasoline filling station. The *Sarah Pecket* was moored to the gasoline pump; while in the cockpit, huddled under his coat, Mr. Pecket lay asleep in the watery rays of the sun just rising above the horizon.

Hearing her moving about, he woke and groaned, stretching his cramped muscles, rubbing his eyes. Then he yawned; afterwards he sneezed. Mary also yawned, for company; following which they stared at each other in embarrassment. "Well," she said finally; "hello."

"Hello," said Mr. Pecket faintly. And he added doubtfully:

"Did you sleep all right?"

"Yes," she said; "sort of." She touched her hips, and winced. "It's a little hard at first," she said. "The wooden beds."

"Bunks," said Mr. Pecket. He tried to rise,

50

but fell back again with a groan. On the second attempt, however, he got himself up. "I made the mooring myself," he explained, "so as not to wake you. Along about six bells in the morning, I should say. Came right up to it."

Mary looked around at the brown autumnal landscape; and then at her elbows. "Where would you say we were?" she asked.

"Hm," said Mr. Pecket. "I wouldn't like to say exactly, not having a chart with me. I've got a chart of the waters off Greenland, but that don't help me right here. I'd say we lay somewheres off Passaic, to judge from the signs."

"Oh," said Mary; and sat down suddenly. Passaic was a long way from Florida. "I'm scared," she said.

And she looked miserably at the filling station. Presently a tear made its way down her cheek. She was cold and hungry; had it really happened? – the sail through the storm, the wind and the rain, the flight across the bridge? It seemed like a dream; she must have been mad. What ever had got into her? She'd lose her job, sure as fate; she'd never be back in time for the morning shift. She had a picture of her own warm, tidy little room, and the bathroom

51

down the hall. "I want to go home," she said.

"Yes, ma'am," said Mr. Pecket gently. "But the wind isn't right for it." He gazed at her with sympathy; he, too, wanted to go home, but he would rather die than admit it. For one thing, it meant giving up the ship....

"I'm headed south," he said stoutly; "I aim to reach latitude thirty, one of these days, and view the Southern Cross."

And catching sight at that moment of the owner of the filling station, Mr. Pecket bellowed at him:

"Ahoy there."

The man came forward with his mouth open. However, he closed it again. He had seen some strange sights in his life, but things always went on as before. "What can I do for you, mister?" he asked; and gave the *Sarah Pecket* a thwack with his palm. When he heard that Mr. Pecket wanted breakfast, he waved his hand at the house. "Come in," he said, "and do your business."

Seated in the kitchen of the filling station, which was also a candy store, lunch-counter, and comfort station, Mr. Pecket and Mary made a good breakfast of coffee, toast, bacon and eggs. The warm room and the hot food cheered their spirits and helped to heal the bruises of the night before. Holding the steaming coffee under his nose, Mr. Pecket exclaimed:

"Well, we're off to a good start."

He continued:

"I'll admit, there were times last night when the wind was almost too much for me. Rounding the turn there, to the bridge.... What I need is more keel, and some reef points. If I could have reefed her down, she'd have handled better."

"What you need," said Mary, "is a good mattress."

"Maybe so," said Mr. Pecket; "maybe so. That's not a question of sailing, rightly speaking. I need more than that; I need a Blue Peter, port and starboard running lights, and a life preserver."

"Go on," said the filling-station owner, "what do you want with a life preserver? What you'd ought to have is a motor."

Mr. Pecket frowned. "I can take a sailboat anywheres, mister," he remarked, "without a motor." He slapped a coin down on the counter. "The lady wants to go home," he said. "I suppose she can get a bus back to the city."

"There's one goes by at seven forty-five," declared the man.

"Then you've got an hour to wait," said

Mr. Pecket. He climbed stiffly down from the counter. "Good-by," he said. "I'm glad to have met you."

She took his hand and pressed it. "You've been awfully good to me," she said. "I hope you don't mind my not going further."

"Not at all," said Mr. Pecket. And he added bravely:

"I'll get along."

"I've got to do the right thing," said Mary. "On account of my job, and all."

"Yes, ma'am," said Mr. Pecket. "Don't you bother your head about me."

"Have a nice trip," she said. "Good-by."

"Good-by," said Mr. Pecket.

"I have to go back," she explained. "On the bus."

"That's right," he agreed. "Well... good-by."

"Good-by," she said. "Have a nice trip. Thank you for everything."

He went slowly out to the *Sarah Pecket* and climbed on board. He felt tired; but the sight of the ship cheered him, tied up there to the pump. It was time to be getting under weigh – time to hoist sail and cast off. The sail was wet, it came up creaking; then he leaned out over the stern, and gave himself a push. The wet sail shone in the light; the fresh wind, blowing over the brown fields, fanned his cheek, warmed by the sun. He took a deep breath, and grasped the wagon-tongue.

A moment later he heard a cry behind him, and looked back to see Mary running down the road after him.

"I've changed my mind, mister," she said, as she climbed on board.

"I'm going with you."

CHAPTER VII

In Which the Sarah Pecket *Gets Her Running Lights.*

Mr. Pecket soon grew used to the road, which seemed to him like what he imagined the sea to be, endless, and gently rolling. The wagon-tongue, protruding behind the vessel, could easily be sawed through, he thought, and then hinged up; set off and connected with a wooden bar, it would make an acceptable tiller. He'd have to do that, first chance he got, for the rope was beginning to blister his fingers. The *Sarah Pecket,* on the other hand, was proving herself a sweet sailer, just as he'd expected, able, even in light airs, to maintain reasonable headway, if the slope were favorable. Downhill she did almost too well – ten to twelve knots, dashing along like a Cup defender. At such times Mr. Pecket grasped the steering rope with all his strength, while Mary held her breath, and crouched in terror on the deck. For what with the sound of wheels, the wind in the

56

sails, the ship creaking and shaking all over, and the loose tackle flapping, they went downhill like thunder. It frightened her at first; but after a while she grew used to it, and even stood up, holding onto the mast, and letting the wind blow past her, as though she were flying.

From time to time cars went by them on the road; people leaned out, craned their necks, gaped at them, waved, and tooted their horns. Mr. Pecket waved back at them like a good sailor; for he believed that one should be friendly and hearty on the water. He watched the sail, handled the wagon-tongue, and tried to teach Mary how to take charge of the stays when the boom swung over. On the open sea a ship wouldn't jibe so much; but on a road, what with the curves and all, he guessed she couldn't very well help herself. For one thing, there wasn't room to come about, in a following wind.

During the course of the morning, he explained to Mary the difference between port and starboard, between sheet and halyard; and how to coil a rope. She thought it very queer, on the whole, but she was willing to learn. Still, why not say left and right, and be done with it? Then other people could tell where you were going. But Mr. Pecket wanted everything to be shipshape

57

and correct on board. "It's a way of speaking," he told her, "for the sea. You have to know it. And another thing: you don't tell the time same as you do on land, either. It goes by bells."

He went on to explain to her what it is that makes a sailboat go. "In this case," he said, "you've got to figure the wheels are like a centerboard or a keel. They keep you going forward, instead of sideways. First of all, you want to see where the wind is coming from. Then you trim your sail to meet it. You want to remember that a boat on the starboard tack has the right of way."

"Well," said Mary, "it's fun, anyhow." She was enjoying herself: even port and starboard seemed easy after a while, and no harder, for that matter, than the things she'd had to learn at the Hollywood Restaurant. "This sail up front has got a split in it," she declared. "I'd sew it for you, if I could get hold of a needle and thread somewheres."

"There's a sewing kit in the cabin," said Mr. Pecket. "But wait a bit before you do it; I've got an idea for changing that sail around a little. I don't rightly need a staysail if the wind's going to be aft our beam most of the time. A flying jib would do me better; or even a spinnaker."

And he added thoughtfully:

58

"What I need most of all is running and riding lights. Only I don't know where I'll get them."

"We could use candles," said Mary helpfully.

Mr. Pecket did not reply to this observation.

"You'll need some other clothes, though," he told her. "You won't be much use on board in a dress like that."

"I could wear an apron," said Mary.

"Well, no," said Mr. Pecket. "I don't hardly think it would do."

He set a course out into the middle of the road, to avoid a low-hanging tree at the roadside. It was pleasant out there; he thought the wind was steadier, too. But he soon discovered that others wanted to get past him. Behind him, a truck let out a blast on its horn. "Hey, you," cried the driver, "you in the tub – move over."

Mr. Pecket moved to the right in a dignified manner, but his feelings were hurt. He had forgotten for a while what it was like to live in a world where people told him to get out of the way; now he was reminded of it again. When he thought how he was, after all, the master of a ship on its way to the Caribbean, it seemed to him that he had a right to ask politeness from people. He would have liked to think of something to say to the driver of the truck as it went by. Look here, he would have liked to say, why not leave other people be, to get along by themselves, without so much pushing and shoving?

However, it was the truck-driver who did the talking, not Mr. Pecket. "Well, well," he said, "my, my. Here's somebody thinks he's sailing on the ocean.

"He's nuts," he explained to his helper on the truck.

"Go home and sail your boat in the bathtub, mister."

The great truck thundered by like a steamer, with a red lantern on one side and a green lantern on the other. The green and red glass shone for a moment in the sunlight; and Mr. Pecket saw it. That's what I ought to have, he thought: lamps like that. He took a deep breath.

"Doggone it," he said –

"You tugboat."

But he was not entirely satisfied with this exchange of sarcasm; and he brooded over it in silence. It was Mary who thought of what to say; although by that time the truck was out of earshot.

"You haven't got a bathtub," she cried after it. "That's your trouble."

And she smiled happily back at Mr.

Pecket, whose face was set and stern. "Never mind," she told him; "they don't know any better."

However, Mr. Pecket's spirits had suffered a temporary setback. He no longer enjoyed watching the sail, or the clouds heaped like pillows in the sky. Instead, he sat huddled over the tiller, thinking about what he would like to have said, if he could have thought of it in time.

The *Sarah Pecket* slipped along, shaking her sails, wallowing a little on the rises; once or twice Mr. Pecket had to get out and push, while Mary took the helm. But for the most part the road was level; and little by little Mr. Pecket's angry feelings subsided, while the clear country air and mellow sun brought about a sense of newness and wonder. These were foreign waters, and he was out to sail them. Even the sky was different from at home, clean and blue, with a dark autumn tone to it, like deep water; it was a sky for travellers, it put distance in the heart. Far off, in the south, the sun-haze deepened above the Carolinas; and Mr. Pecket breathed the Jersey air, tasting in his mouth already the flavor of spice and hemp, and the salt wind of the sea; already, in his mind, smelling the off-shore breeze, drowsy and sweet, a little warm, a little rotten.

61

That afternoon, bearing always southward, he left the foothills of the Ramapos and Oranges behind him; and viewed at his feet the level plains of the Elizabeths. And it was here, rounding a turn in the westering sun, that he saw before him the truck which had passed him a few hours earlier on the road. Parked in front of a lunchroom, in which the driver and his helper were eating their lunch, it stood by the roadside empty and motionless, an abandoned hulk, a deserted derelict. Quietly, smiling a little to himself, Mr. Pecket sailed past; and brought the *Sarah Pecket* to a stop a little distance farther on. He knew what he had to do. Bidding Mary watch the ship, he armed himself with a screwdriver and a monkey-wrench, and returned on foot to the truck.

It would be a pity, he thought, not to make the most of such an opportunity.

In a little while he was back on board again, his course set once more for the south.

That night the *Sarah Pecket* rode through the darkness with red and green running lights at her port and starboard quarters. And Mr. Pecket, at the helm, lifted his face to the stars, to where, some day, the Southern Cross would be, strung across the sky. He was not sorry for what he had done.

He told himself that he was glad that he had been able to salvage something.

CHAPTER VIII

Mr. Williams Comes Overside.

"Oh, rolling down to Rio,
We're rolling down to Rio," sang Mr. Pecket; and breathed the cool fresh air.

The *Sarah Pecket* was staggering down a long swell of road through the farm lands of Pennsylvania. In front of him, forward of the mast, sat Mary; dressed in an old pair of overalls, she was perched tidily on the windlass, sewing a patch on the jib, which had been torn in the storm, and which Mr. Pecket hoped to convert from time to time into a spinnaker. Below, in the cabin, a pot of soup simmered on the stove built from an alcohol lamp, a piece of grill, and a tin packing case. Mr. Pecket was happy; his face was thinner, but it had color. Mary, on the other hand, had begun to fill out a little. The life agreed with her; she slept well, and she had taken to eating again. It was too late in the year for sunburn, but her cheeks were pink, like little apples.

Mr. Pecket had only one complaint to make: he felt that Mary kept the ship too neat. He had no desire to own a yacht; what he wanted was a sailboat, something simple and briny. However, Mary had her own ideas of what a boat ought to look like. A steam yacht would have suited her very well, but she was adaptable; on the other hand, she had no intention of arriving in Florida in an oyster barge.

"Because," she told him, "the first thing people do is notice what you look like. They don't stop to ask are you a lady."

"What difference does it make?" asked Mr. Pecket. "Ladies aren't happier than anybody else."

"They mayn't be happier," Mary answered, "but they're better off. You can have a lot of pleasure by yourself, if you're a lady."

Mr. Pecket considered this carefully before replying. After a while he remarked:

"Maybe you don't like sailing."

He continued inexorably:

"A good sailor never meddles with other people's lives. He can leave them be as God made them, because all he asks for himself is leeway and headway. So if you want to be a lady, I don't object; all I say is, get the jib sheeted down first."

"Talk English," said Mary. "What'll I do with the jib?"

"Fasten it to the deck," said Mr. Pecket moodily.

He gazed about him at the rolling fields, beneath which the earth, moving through her seasons, seemed to rise and fall in never-ending waves, majestic as the sea, but more friendly. "You'd think," he said, "that farmers would be like sailors, and mind their own business; but on the contrary. Farms breed as meddlesome a lot of people as are to be found anywhere, I don't know why."

"The thing is," said Mary, "you get to thinking on a farm."

"Yes," said Mr. Pecket; "but what about?"

"You think about how to better yourself," she said.

But Mr. Pecket was not satisfied with this explanation. "Well, no, as a matter of fact," he said, "it's bettering others that people on farms do most of their thinking about. Wanting to better your neighbor is just another way of saying he don't amount to much the way he is.

"You won't find that kind of thing at sea."

And he added:

"The wind has changed; I'm going to jibe her over."

"Go ahead," said Mary; "don't mind me, I'm forward."

But she lay down on deck anyway, to be sure.

"Look out for your head," said Mr. Pecket. He swung the *Sarah Pecket* a bit to port, the sail went over with a rattle, and the vessel listed comfortably to starboard. "There goes a pelican across our bow," he remarked.

Cawing bleakly, the pelican flapped past and lighted in a tree at the edge of a field, where he looked very much like a crow. The *Sarah Pecket*, with the wind on her beam, scuttled along at a fair pace; and Mr. Pecket was satisfied. At sea he would have lashed the wheel, and gone below, but the winding road made such a course unsafe. Instead, he called for Mary to relieve him at the tiller. "Here," he said, "stand watch for a while; I'm going below, to look after the soup and snatch a wink of sleep. Call me at four bells."

"All right," said Mary; "I will."

Mr. Pecket sighed; he would have liked her to say: "Ay, ay, sir."

"Well," he said vaguely, "make it so"; and went down the four little steps to the cabin.

Mary grasped the tiller, and bent her gaze upon the road ahead. She felt peaceful and hearty; the easy motion of the ship, wafted steadily southward by the winds, encouraged her to trust in providence and in her own powers. She felt that there was time for everything, that everything was in its proper place and moving quietly toward its destiny. It is part of that feeling of ocean known to the sailor, that restfulness of the sea, upon which the hopes of man move in their gentle courses, like dreams of the child on the breast of the mother.

Southward the haze of autumn deepened over Panama and Delaware; the shadows lengthened along the road. The *Sarah Pecket* floated on the wind toward Florida and the blue waters of the Gulf, while the breezes, spilling from her sails, passed on across the fields and woods and lost themselves above the gray Atlantic. And Mary, her hand on the tiller, dreamed not of boats, but of goodness, and roses, and an ermine coat.

The road, curving, hid from her sight the young man and the pushcart until she was almost on top of him. Then it was too late; taken by surprise, she thrust the tiller hard to starboard, the sail jibed over to port, catching her head as it went by, and carrying the wagon-tongue along with it back to port again. The *Sarah Pecket* wavered, veered, and skating back across the road, hurled herself like a frigate at the young man and his cart, tossing them both into the ditch with a crash which could be heard over half the countryside.

A moment later Mr. Pecket appeared on deck, with his mouth open. "We've hit something," he said. "Belay there."

And seeing the young man sitting in the ditch, he added,

"Ahoy."

Upset, and taken by surprise, the young man could not think of anything to say. But presently he exclaimed: "Who do you think you are?"

Mr. Pecket gazed down at him with interest and sympathy. "I'm Cap'n Hector Pecket of the sloop *Sarah Pecket*," he said, "four days out of New York, and Florida bound. I'm sorry we ran afoul of you, mister; the wind's tricky in these latitudes."

The young man eyed him moodily. "What's the matter with you?" he asked. "Can't you look where you're going?"

"Not very good," said Mr. Pecket apologetically, "on account of the sail. However, I'll be glad to help you get your things stowed back in the cart again, just as soon as I loose this main sheet."

And turning to Mary, he exclaimed:

"Stir yourself, Kelly, or you'll have us over on our side in a minute."

All he received by way of answer was a groan. Mary was huddled in the cockpit, holding her head which had been smacked by the boom. "Go away," she said: "don't talk to me. I've killed myself."

Mr. Pecket loosed the main sheet by himself; then he climbed down over the ship's side to help the young man pick up his belongings, which consisted of several boxes and bags, a roll of bedding, and a grindstone. "I still think I ought to take a poke at you," said the young man. "I would, too, for three cents."

Mr. Pecket paid no attention to these remarks. "Here," he said, "help me to right this wagon of yours. The wheel's cracked."

These words caused the young man to gaze at his cart in dismay. "What am I going to do now?" he said. "I ask you."

To this Mr. Pecket made no immediate reply; he was examining the wheel, and figuring things out in his head. "I could put a new rim on it for you," he said finally, "or fix the old one with wire and glue. That would hold, but not for long." Straightening up, he favored the young man with a thoughtful glance. "Where are you bound

70

for, mister?" he asked. "What port of call?"

The young man replied that he was headed nowhere in particular and that he was bound wherever there was business. "I'm on my way south," he said. And he pointed to a sign on the side of his cart, which read:

H. Williams, Dentist. Teeth Filled. Knives and Scissors Ground.

"You've put me out of business," he declared. "I can't go anywheres without my cart."

"Well, now," said Mr. Pecket, "you can't, and that's a fact." He scratched his chin thoughtfully. "I could take you along with me a ways," he said, "if that would suit you. We'd be a little crowded, maybe, but I guess I wouldn't mind."

Then it was Mr. Williams's turn to scratch his chin. He looked at Mr. Pecket; and he looked at the boat. "Is there room for me and my grinder?" he asked.

"I guess maybe we could fit it into the cockpit," said Mr. Pecket. And turning to the ship, he called out:

"You, Kelly – give us a hand."

"Go away," said Mary. "Don't bother me."

"Well, come along, mister," said Mr. Pecket. "It's you and me."

But Mr. Williams had already gone over

to the ship, and was looking down at Mary, who was sitting on the floor, holding her head. "So you're Kelly," he remarked. "Well, you ought to look out where you're going."

She lifted her face, red with the bump, and stained with tears. "Miss Kelly, to you," she declared.

Mr. Williams smiled, for the first time that morning. "All right," he said to Mr. Pecket. "Let's get going."

CHAPTER IX

In Which Mary Plays the Part of a Lady.

"What I'd like to do," said Mr. Williams, "is head north for Greenland, and see is pemmican good for the teeth like they say."

"She wouldn't stand the ice," said Mr. Pecket.

They were resting on the shores of the Chesapeake. At their backs stood the *Sarah Pecket*, with laundry hanging from her lines, drying in the sun. Mary was sleeping in the cabin, before taking over the afternoon watch; below them stretched the blue waters of the bay, ruffled by the wind, bright in the noonday light. The pine trees of the shore filled their noses with fragrance, mixed with the smoky odors of earth and the cool smell of water. Mr. Pecket was thinking of his wife Sarah; he did not regret her absence, though he wished she could have been there to see how much he was enjoying himself. During the day he was busy plotting the ship's course, trimming sail, or making the many

73

repairs which were needed to keep the vessel right side up; and at night he fell asleep like a man of action, without thinking about death, or anything unpleasant. When it was his turn to take over the night watch, he looked upward at the stars, letting his mind float at peace among the frosty currents of the sky, or explored in imagination the quiet depths of the heavens, like a diver the deeps of ocean. How good life is, he thought, if only a man is given leave to live it. Each for himself, and all for God, that's how it ought to be. But that's not how it is. O meddlesome, brief world. ... What people need, he thought, is to respect each other more, and leave each other be. Let each man own his ship, and sail it where he likes.

Yes, he thought, all men should be sailors, for that was the only way not to be lonely in the world. Perhaps there were some who kept to their homes out of love; but then, it must be love kept them there. He sighed, and for a moment his eyes grew cloudy. Love – that must have been something he'd missed in the world, like Melville Bay. He tried to think when Sarah had ever kissed him, but he couldn't remember. He didn't think he'd ever thought of it before.

"No," he remarked, "I'd like to see the northern lights. But the *Sarah* wasn't built for ice. She'd do better in the south, where it's warm."

"There's money in things for the teeth," said Mr. Williams. He was still thinking about pemmican, although he did not expect to see any. But he expected to make his way in the world before very long. It was this which had caused him to add a grindstone to his effects, in order to have something to do in towns where there were already plenty of dentists. "You've got to use your wits to get along in the world," he said; and sighed for eagerness to have a chance to use them.

Mr. Pecket played for a moment with the idea of a fortune, and then put it from him. "What would I do with riches," he demanded, "more than what I'm doing? I can see that plain enough, now that I've left the city. It's only there that you spend your time worrying about money, because people have a money look about them. What do you buy, what do you sell? ... But here, like on the sea, you've got the sun and the wind free, and all you need is food and an overcoat. I couldn't be better off in a new set of clothes than I am this minute."

And he stretched himself gratefully in the sun.

Mr. Williams also enjoyed the sun; but he believed that there was something else in life.

75

For instance, he saw himself with money in the bank, and an office on the door of which was a sign saying: Dr. Henry Williams, Dentist. It had been a mistake to leave his home in Iowa, and the little dental college from which he had received a degree; but what was he to do? Iowa was full of dentists, and so was the east; he'd have done better to take up farming – that is, if he'd had a farm. Not that he felt much like a doctor, pushing a cart around; but he wasn't one to do nothing; and you never could tell.

"Yes sir," he said, "I don't aim to be poor all my life. But you take yourself, now – you talk like you were an old man. It surprises me, because you look healthier than you sound."

Mr. Pecket was hurt; but then it occurred to him that perhaps Mr. Williams was right, after all. When you're young, he thought, everybody else seems old; but when you're old, it's just the other way around, then everybody else seems young. And he remembered how, when he was a child, to be twelve seemed to him to be almost a grown man. A boy of twelve had a few good things, like a man had: a watch, a knife – he didn't need all the bits of wood and string a child needed. And he went on to consider how, little by little, a man gets to do without things he doesn't need. Somewhere along in there, he told himself, is the place a man isn't young any more, but I don't know just exactly where it is. It's like it is with a child, there's nothing so small or so far but what he'll reach for it. When he grows up, he gets to see what's too trifling, or too far off; and after a while what he's done and what he's got seem almost enough for him. That's when he's old: that's when the afternoon begins to slide downhill into evening. It's not long after that before it's time to sleep, and it doesn't matter any more what he got for himself, or didn't get – he leaves it all behind him, anyway.

He shivered a little in the cool water-breeze; for these reflections led him to think about his wife, who had wanted to turn the *Sarah Pecket* into a lunch-counter, and from whom he had run away. He thought that she was surely angry, and perhaps lonely ... when you were old, that was when you wanted to be alone. But was she old? Sarah, with her schemes? ... And was he? There was still Greenland, and the Bay of Naples, before the long afternoon slid into evening, before it was time to fold his hands, and see the *Sarah Pecket* standing there, still and quiet, like a lunchroom. . . .

"No, sir," he said to Mr. Williams, "don't

mistake me, just because I'm satisfied with what I've got. You haven't heard my sea-voice yet; wait a bit, you'll see am I healthy or not."

And casting a weather eye aloft, he inquired of the sky its plans for the morrow.

The sun rippled across the waters of the bay, the breeze stirred in the pines; and Mr. Williams rose to his feet and went in search of his grindstone. He felt active; and he thought that he would like to make use of the afternoon to sharpen a few of his instruments. As he worked, he sang, for joy, and for youth, and because there was already so much noise from the grindstone. Presently the scuttle of the cabin opened, and Mary put out her head, moody with sleep. "My goodness," she said, "do you have to do that?"

Mr. Williams replied that he was preparing for the future. "I've got to get ready for my patients," he said. "They might be along any time now."

"Well," said Mary. "I was only resting myself a little."

And she added in a modest way,

"Life on a boat is so exciting."

From the bank below, Mr. Pecket called up to her: "You, Kelly – see can you tighten that forward stay. She'll snap the mast right out of her one of these days."

"O.K.," said Mary; and then bit her tongue. Why did she always have to use the wrong kind of language? What was it sailors said? "Perdon me," she remarked to Mr. Williams, "I got to go forward."

But there was nothing she could do with the forward stay, and she returned to Mr. Williams again. "I guess it'll have to do like it is," she said to him. "I guess I can't fix it."

"Me neither," said Mr. Williams. "I don't even know what he's talking about, half the time."

Mary laughed lightly. "You'll get used to it," she assured him. "It takes a little while."

"Well," said Mr. Williams, "what's a forward stay?"

"It's the thing that holds the mast out front," said Mary, "that the jib runs up on." And she blushed with pride to know so much, and explain it so clearly.

"I come from farming country," said Mr. Williams, "I was never taught sailboating."

"Oh well," said Mary, "it comes easy. It's just the names get you mixed up at first."

It pleased her to imagine herself at home in a world of flying jibs and spinnakers.

Looking at him from out the corner of her eye, she wondered what he was thinking about. Did he, perhaps, mistake her for a sailor? Well, she'd let him; it wouldn't do him any harm to respect her a little. "I can't do much with that stay, skipper," she called out to Mr. Pecket; "you'll just have to ease your sheet a little on the thank-you-marms."

She gave her hair a twist and a pat. "It's lovely weather for sailing," she said; "my."

And she hummed a little tune to herself.

Mr. Williams poured some water onto the grindstone. Then he tested the point of a scraper against his palm, and began grinding. "The old man says," he declared, pumping with his foot, "we'll be across the line in a week. What line, I asked him, but he didn't say."

"I guess he meant the line between the north and south," said Mary. She clapped her hands softly together. "We'll really be in the south then," she said. "Have you ever been in the south, Mr. Williams?"

Mr. Williams squinted at the scraper in his hand. "Look," he said; "don't call me that, will you? Call me Henry."

"Excuse me," said Mary. "Were you ever in the south, then, Henry?"

"Well," said Mr. Williams, beginning to
80

tread his grindstone again, "I've been in Virginia. It's nice country. Sort of red, underfoot."

"Did you see the palm trees?" asked Mary.

"I can't say I did," he replied. "Should I ought to have?"

"I don't know," said Mary; "a friend of mine told me about them. I've seen palm trees in the movies."

"I guess I wasn't there long enough," said Mr. Williams. "But it smells nice. I like a nice, sweet-smelling country, myself; I come from one. There wasn't much work, so I came north."

Mary sighed; she would have liked to talk about her chances of finding work in Florida, but it seemed out of place, considering what she was supposed to be. "I guess work is hard to find," she said. "Anyone who had a job would be a fool to leave it."

And she gave a gasp, thinking of how she had done that very thing herself.

Mr. Williams nodded. "That's a fact," he said. "Work is hard to get. But don't worry; my chance will come along. I aim to take my time, and have a good look-around first; then, when I see what I like . . ."

And with an expressive gesture, he placed the scraper against the stone.

81

"That's because you're a man," said Mary. "With a girl, it's different. She's got to take what she can get."

"Sure," said Mr. Williams carelessly; "a girl's got to be glad for whatever comes along."

"Of course," said Mary without much hope, "she doesn't have to stay in one place, necessarily."

However, Mr. Williams thought differently. "In my opinion," he remarked, "it's a mistake for a girl to go spreading herself around."

"Oh," said Mary.

"It's like this," said Mr. Williams. "A girl looks best at home. So the best thing she can do is stay there."

"But," said Mary faintly, "suppose nothing ever comes along for her?"

Mr. Williams shrugged his shoulders. "Ask me something easy," he said. "I'm just telling you how it is."

The sun shone, and the grindstone sang; and Mary looked down over the boat's side to where the blue windy water broke against the shore in little ripples. She didn't know whether to be happy or sad, whether to smile or frown. She thought that she didn't care for Mr. Williams very much, he was so sure he knew everything; and besides, what if he found out that she was a waitress, and not a lady? Though why a waitress shouldn't be a lady as well...and then, all that about staying at home; it was so like a man, to know what was best for a woman....

It was like a man to think he knew it all. As though a girl oughtn't to travel, if she had the chance; as though she oughtn't to better herself if she could. Oh no, mister, she thought, a girl could stay at home and die of it, for all you'd care. But not me; I've got other things to do.

Nevertheless, something sang inside her; and her mouth curved in a smile. It's such a fine day, she told herself, that's what's the matter. And tomorrow – or next week –

We'll be in the south. Oh glory.

CHAPTER X

In Which the Sarah Pecket *Takes on a Cargo of Contraband.*

Shouldering the air, her light sails drawing full, the *Sarah Pecket* thundered south through Maryland on the wings of a northerly wind. Mr. Pecket had set his spinnaker, and Mary had stitched him a topsail out of burlap; Mr. William's cart bobbed along behind him in place of a dinghy, a small American flag fluttering from its stern. The topsail, sent up in stops, broke out overhead with a sound like a cannon, and the vessel raced southward, followed by some sparrows who were also making the trip.

The three travellers spelled each other at the helm; at night they cast anchor near a convenient comfort station, or in the open fields, watched by the stars and by the little creatures of the darkness. Occasionally a car would go roaring past them on the road, like a rocket, but that was another life, they hardly noticed such things. Instead, they watched the towns and villages drift slowly by, like degrees of latitude, or contemplated the night-time sky, which, to Mr. Pecket at least, was a source of never-ending wonder.

He could not forget that the stars he saw were so much larger than the sun, which already was too big for him to conceive of. And among those stars were others he could not even see, and still others beyond, out to the ends of space, of which, however, there was no end. Such thoughts induced in Mr. Pecket a feeling of humbleness and confusion, which was very comforting. For if there was no end to space, then that end might just as well be right there beside him, on the deck of the *Sarah Pecket* – a fact which caused him to lose his breath whenever he thought about it.

It is such thoughts as this which give the sailor his air of modesty, courage, and perplexity. But the farmer, who also views, day after day, an endless vista of earth, sky, and cloud effects, goes indoors as soon as it gets dark, and fixes his mind on his accounts. He is a business man, and in the midst of plenty he is obliged to curtail his production, in order to keep his prices up. Since nature herself takes a hand in this production, he can never be sure where he stands.

Mr. Ora Menaby, whose farm lay south

of Baltimore, was allowed by the government to sell ten calves, and no more. However, a young cow, unable to help herself, had just presented him with another calf, one over his allotment. Mr. Menaby was, as he put it, in a pickle. He knew that he could sell the new arrival to his cousin Ralph, in Virginia; but, on the other hand, had he a right to do it? And how to get it there, with nobody the wiser, left him stumped. He didn't trust his neighbors not to tell on him, any more than he'd expect not to tell on them, if he had the chance.

It was while he was puzzling over this problem, and thinking soberly of the seven dollars he could expect to get for the calf, that Mr. Pecket drew up to his door, in search of milk. Mr. Menaby went to the gate and stood there looking at the ship. He had never seen anything just like it; it made him think of the ocean. That was the way one sent things abroad – by sea: cotton, livestock, and merchandise; or down from Philadelphia and Boston.

"That's a handsome wagon you've got there, stranger," he said at last. "It looks like a boat to me." He gazed with admiration at the cart, set on behind. "Yes, sir," he said, "that's a cute contraption."

"I guess it is," said Mr. Pecket happily.

86

There was a ring of milk around his mouth, and he sighed from having drunk so fast. "She'll get me where I'm going," he said, smacking his lips. "That's good milk, mister."

"It ought to be," said Mr. Menaby, to whom milk was nothing new. "How far are you going?" he asked.

"No more than around the world," answered Mr. Pecket, "by way of Florida."

He waved his hand at Mary and Mr. Williams. "There's the crew," he said. "One of them's a dentist."

"Pleased to meet you, I'm sure," said Mary politely.

Mr. Menaby looked thoughtful. "You've got a long ways yet to go," he said. "A long, long ways."

He glanced carefully up and down the road. "My wife could make use of a dentist," he said, "if you'd care to light. That is, if you're in no hurry. And seeing as how you aim to circumnavigate the globe, I'd say you had plenty of time."

Before he had finished talking, Mr. Williams had gathered his tools together. "Happy to oblige," he said, clambering briskly over the ship's side. "Wait for me, skipper."

Mr. Menaby conducted him indoors, and

87

then returned to join Mary and Mr. Pecket. "Yes sir," he said, "you've got a long ways to go. You'd better come in and sit down awhile."

But Mr. Pecket was tired of sitting. "Maybe you'll let us walk over your farm," he said to Mr. Menaby. "I never did see a farm, I don't think."

"I'd like to look at the animals," said Mary. She saw herself under an apple tree, with her arms around a horse or a cow, or walking by the side of a stream, driving the geese or the sheep. She was waiting for somebody, and her sunbonnet had fallen down over her shoulders. It was spring, and the trees were covered with apple blossoms.

They went to see the well, and what was left of the truck garden, the frames, and the pile of hay and dung for spring fertilizer. A few chickens ran along before their feet; the air was mild and smoky, watery and cool, it smelled of milk and dead leaves. When they got to the barn, Mr. Menaby stopped. "Well now," he said, "that's a funny thing." And he told them about the new calf, and the trouble he was having over it. "It's the law," he said, "has got me mad. There's seven dollars waiting for that calf in Beaver Dam, Virginia, and the law says No, I can't have it."

Mr. Pecket shook his head. "It seems a pity," he said.

"That's what I said to my wife just yesterday," said Mr. Menaby. "'It's a pity,' I said to her; 'and my cousin Ralph Menaby down in Beaver Dam, Virginia, fair itching for that calf, and all I have to do is get it to him.'"

And he shot Mr. Pecket a shrewd glance out of the corner of his eye.

Mary leaned over the side of the stall and looked down at the calf, who came hopefully forward, and put out his stubby little head to be scratched. "Moo," he said; and Mary gave a jump. "Goodness," she cried. "He spoke to me."

She patted the small brown neck, sinewy and firm, and new in the world. "I wish we could have a little cow like that," she said.

"Well," said Mr. Menaby, "maybe we could fix it so you could."

It was what he had been working toward; he had had it in his mind from the first. "You're going through Virginia," he said, "one way or another."

And he went on to suggest that they take the calf on their cart, and deliver it to his cousin near Beaver Dam. "I've arranged to pay this dentist friend of yours a dollar when he's done," he told them, "and there's seven for the calf, to be collected. I trust you; you look like honest folk to me. Give me a dollar down, and take the calf along with you; and I'll give the dentist two dollars instead of one, to be collected in Beaver Dam from my cousin Ralph, along with the dollar you've given me."

"But what if your cousin Ralph doesn't want it?" asked Mr. Pecket sensibly.

"Then you've got the calf," declared Mr. Menaby, "and I'm the loser. But he'll want it, all right." He forgot to add that his cousin Ralph was in the meat business.

Mr. Pecket looked dubious. "My ship's no cattle boat," he said.

"Well, no," agreed Mr. Menaby. "I can see that. But then, this little animal is more like a pet, so to speak."

"That's true," said Mr. Pecket. "Cap'n Slocum took an animal onto his boat the *Spray*. He took a goat, if I remember rightly. Well, I don't know, mister. Where's Beaver Dam?"

"Right in your path," said Mr. Menaby, "more or less, or no more than a few miles out."

Mary leaned down and put her arms around the calf's neck. The little animal stood still for a moment, licking her overalls with his hard, rough tongue. Then he

90

wriggled away, and tried to butt her. "You're going along with us," she said. "Are you glad, you funny little calf?"

And turning to Mr. Pecket, she exclaimed:

"I couldn't stand to leave him."

But Mr. Pecket was uneasy in his mind.

"I don't know about this," he said. "After all, it's Henry's money. It seems to me he ought to have a say in it."

"Of course," said Mr. Menaby thoughtfully, "I could slaughter this little calf myself. I could just as easy cut its throat, or hit it over the head with an ax."

"Oh," said Mary.

"Yes ma'am," continued Mr. Menaby. "There's tasty veal in that calf, government or no government."

Mary's eyes grew round; her arms tightened convulsively about the little creature's neck.

"Oh no," she said.

"Never.

"I won't let you be veal," she told the calf.

And she cast a glance full of appeal at Mr. Pecket.

Mr. Pecket returned the glance with a look of uncertainty. "Is your heart set on this thing, Kelly?" he asked her.

91

"It is," she said.

"All right," he said, with a sigh. "Bring it along, and we'll stow it in the dinghy."

Thus it was that Mr. Williams found a calf instead of a dollar waiting for him when he came out of the house. He was very angry. "That was my money, not yours," he said, "I'll have you know."

Ho, thought Mr. Pecket, I was afraid of that.

"Maybe it was your money," said Mary, "but just the same, we doubled it for you."

"I don't need you to double my money for me," said Mr. Williams. "I can double my own money."

And folding his arms, he assumed a truculent pose.

"Besides," said Mary, "it'll give us milk on the way, and that's a big saving."

Mr. Pecket interposed mildly: "It looks sort of young to me, for milk."

"Milk?" said Mr. Williams. "From that?" He looked back at the cart, on which the calf, thoroughly hobbled and miserable, behind a little pile of hay, swayed and bobbed uncertainly on its slightly knock-kneed legs. While he gazed, the animal let out a low, plaintive bleat. "Don't moo at me," said Mr. Williams bitterly, pointing at Mary. "Moo at her."

And with a set and gloomy face, he descended to the cabin, and threw himself upon his bunk. He had wanted that dollar to buy a white jacket for himself, to wear in his office.

The *Sarah Pecket,* her nose pointing once more to the south, slipped along in the mellow autumn air, her blocks rattling, and her timbers creaking. The cotton sails were full of wind, they drew her on, lurching a little from side to side, bobbing over the rises. And behind her in the dinghy, lonely and protesting, followed the little calf whose life, barely begun, was already almost finished.

CHAPTER XI

A Storm at Sea.

Mr. Pecket felt like a business man. It seemed to him that he had made a successful financial turn, a fact which caused him to see the entire country in a different light. He began to imagine what he would do if he had a lot of money; for one thing, it did not seem so unlikely any more. And how rosy that made everything. With new eyes, and with a feeling of happiness and goodwill, he looked about him at the houses, the fields, and the filling stations owned by men like himself; like himself, they had been able to make two dollars grow where there had only been one before. And with a heart bursting with pride, he called out in a loud voice:

"Ease that spinnaker boom, and sheet her home."

"Goodness," said Mary under her breath, "what does he mean?"

And putting her head down the forward scuttle, she peered anxiously into the fo'-

c'sle. "What's he mean, Henry?" she asked; "'sheet her home'?"

"How do I know?" replied Mr. Williams angrily.

"Well, you needn't bark at me," said Mary; and withdrawing her head in a hurry, she went in search of the skipper. "What was it you wanted me to do?" she asked him.

However, Mr. Pecket had forgotten. "Never mind," he said; "I was just thinking. It's not so hard to be a business man, Kelly. It's a matter of having the right ideas about things."

"Yes," said Mary. "Did you want me to do anything about the spinnaker?"

Mr. Pecket cocked an eye forward. "No," he said, "she's drawing all right as she is. What I mean," he continued, "is this: look how easy I doubled that money we got from Mr. Menaby."

"We haven't got it yet," said Mary. "It's at Beaver Dam, waiting. And anyhow, it was Henry's money."

"That's just it," said Mr. Pecket eagerly. "That's what makes it business. It's got me thinking, Kelly. Maybe you've got to do things with other people's money, to be a business man. I never did anything with my own money, but lose it. I had no head for it; that's what my wife always said."

"So you've got a wife," said Mary slowly.

"I have," said Mr. Pecket. "I ran away from her."

Mary shook her head. "Oh Mr. Pecket," she exclaimed, "had you ought to have?"

"Maybe not," replied Mr. Pecket, "but it's done now, and I don't regret it. After I've been around the world a little, I'll go home and settle down. She wants to sell my boat to a butcher."

Mary put her hand ever so lightly on his arm. "I'm sorry," she said. "But is it right? I mean, what you're doing – running away like this? Maybe she thinks you're dead, poor woman. Maybe she's unhappy, all alone, wondering."

The sun seemed less bright to Mr. Pecket, who suddenly felt his heart contract. "Do you think so?" he asked.

"Well," said Mary, "I'd be in a fine state, if it was me. Don't you think maybe you ought to at least write her a letter, and tell her where you are?"

"Maybe I ought," said Mr. Pecket in a small voice. "I'll think about it."

He was not as happy as he had been. It was strange, how thinking about Sarah made everything look the way it used to, at home. Could she really be worrying about him? He had never even considered such a possibility.

That she would be angry, he did not doubt...but that she might miss him? He felt startled; and at the same time a little frightened. The old fears came back with a rush – the busy city, the unfriendly faces, a world of anxiety. Yes, that's the way it was; he had forgotten. He found himself glancing at the sky for weather signs. There was a flood coming some day, to wash the world clean again...he'd forgotten that too, come to think of it. Not tomorrow, to judge by the sky; though he didn't like the look of things in the south-west.

"Kelly," he said, "you'd best get the tops' down. And tell Henry to take in the spinnaker boom, and set the jib. I don't feel easy in my mind any more."

Mary looked back over the stern at the trailer. "What'll we do with the cow?" she asked. "He's not eating his hay."

"He's too small," said Mr. Pecket. "I should have asked the farmer what to feed him. Maybe what he wants is milk. We'll stop somewheres and get a bottle."

"If we have to feed him milk," said Mary soberly, "we won't come out so well."

"Well, no," agreed Mr. Pecket unhappily, "we won't."

"Do you think the farmer knew that, when he said would we take him?" asked Mary.

"I wouldn't put it past him," said Mr. Pecket.

"I guess business is harder than you thought," said Mary.

"I guess maybe it is," said Mr. Pecket.

They stopped that evening for supper at a lunchroom outside of Washington. The wind was rising, and the air felt cold and unsteady. Weather was making; the *Sarah Pecket* was already staggering a little in the gusts. They lowered sail, and went inside, to get milk for the calf, and hamburgers, coffee, and apple pie for themselves. In addition, Mr. Pecket ordered a glass of beer, for he felt that he needed cheering.

It was while he was drinking his beer that he noticed the woman at the counter beside him. Large, gray, and severe, she was looking at him in a frank and critical way. She saw his clothes, which were a good deal the worse for a full week's sailing; and she looked at his nose, sunk in the beery foam. "Some people," she remarked, "ought to be ashamed of themselves."

Mr. Pecket was startled. Then he glanced around, to see if anybody else had been addressed. But no one else was there; Mary and Mr. Williams were seated together at the other end of the counter. He looked back at the woman, whose eyes, over a dish of vegetables, were fixed with a stony expression upon his glass of beer. "For they know not what they do," she said.

"Were you talking to me?" asked Mr. Pecket.

"I was," said the woman. "You ought to hide your head in shame over what you're doing."

Mr. Pecket looked at the glass in his hand; he gave it a turn and watched the foam rise like a wave. "Don't you like beer?" he asked.

"I do not," said the woman.

And drawing from her handbag a little tract, she presented it to Mr. Pecket, who received it with hesitation. *How Beer*, he read, *Destroys the Home. By Mrs. Myra Hawkins.*

"It's not too late, mister," she declared. "There's still time to take thought."

Mr. Pecket gazed moodily into his glass, amber, and flecked with foam. Then he drained it off and set it down on the counter. He was not at all used to beer; it made him feel more cheerful, and at the same time a little dizzy. "Fill her up again," he told the counterman. And leaning toward the lady at his side, he remarked confidentially:

"Beer is vegetables."

"Beer is not vegetables," said Mrs. Hawkins. "Beer is alcohol."

"I don't believe it," said Mr. Pecket.

He drank his second beer without a stop; after which he gave a gasp. "Fill her up again," he told the counterman when he'd got his breath; "I don't like nosy people."

And he added, wiping his lips with the back of his hand:

"I never did like them very much."

"It's a sad thing," said Mrs. Hawkins, "to see a strong man in the throes of drink."

"Go away," said Mr. Pecket. He felt brave; though at the same time quiet and comfortable. "You and your vegetables."

The woman heaved a sigh. "In the throes of drink," she said resolutely. "It's a sickening sight."

"It's not me is a sickening sight," said Mr. Pecket. He was half way through his third glass; it no longer had any taste to it, but he meant to down it, no matter what. "I'm Cap'n Hector Pecket of the sloop – the sloop *Sarah Pecket* – of New York," he declared. "And that's my crew over there in the corner. One of them's a dentist. I can't see which one. You believe me, don't you?"

"You're destroying your soul," said Mrs. Hawkins, "and the lining of your stomach."

"The lining of my stomach," said Mr.

Pecket, taking his nose out of the foam, "is made of stomach. Nobody can destroy it."

With these words he brought up a hearty belch. "There you are," he said.

The author of *How Beer Destroys the Home* turned pale and pushed her plate away. "You're on the road to hell, mister," she said. "That's what you're on the road to."

"Well," said Mr. Pecket, "you don't look so good yourself, neither."

And throwing some coins onto the counter, he rose to his feet and moved majestically but somewhat uncertainly toward the door. "Up sail," he bellowed, "and away – away – from here."

He staggered out into the air. Mary and Mr. Williams went out after him; they helped him over the side, and got the sail up, though not without misgivings. "We'd ought to anchor," said Mary, "with this wind, and all." It was true; the wind had grown stronger, and the *Sarah Pecket* heeled over as she started down the road. Mr. Pecket suddenly felt very sleepy. He was having a little trouble keeping Mary's face from swimming away to where he couldn't see it any more. The motion of the boat was not unpleasant, it was like a rocking-chair. But everything was cloudy. People were nosy; but he'd told them off. What a man he was, when all was said and done – when all was said and done. Those were good-sounding words; he'd have to repeat them to Sarah some time. Unfortunately, his stomach felt swollen. However, he thought it would hold. Time to sleep, now.

He lifted his head and stared at Mary through the wind and the murk. "Am I a sickening sight?" he asked her.

"Not to my knowledge," she answered, straining at the port stay.

"Me neither," said Mr. Pecket; and fell asleep.

Mr. Williams lowered him into the cabin and laid him out on the bunk. Then he climbed up again and relieved Mary at the helm. The ship was running fast, well over on her beam; they should have let the mainsail out, but neither of them thought of it. The wind was beginning to sing in the canvas and whine in the tackle; they were going too fast for comfort. Mr. Williams hung onto the helm and closed his eyes; he felt frightened. "Oh cripes," he groaned, "what'll we do?"

"Give it to me," said Mary. "I'll take it."

She felt suddenly brave and able; the wind did not frighten her any longer. She was the captain now, a woman – all woman – against the storm. Nobody else could help her, and she needed nobody. She knew the wind, she was part of it; she could ride it, she could ride it out. Any woman could, if she had to; it was only a man broke in two at a blow. "Henry," she said, "get that cow in here, and put him in the cabin with the skipper. He'll get bumped back there, sure as shooting. Here's a curve coming; look out for your head."

Over went the boom against the port stay, but the *Sarah Pecket* held her course. In the cabin the limp form of Mr. Pecket rolled from one side of the bunk to the other; and Mr. Williams, holding his breath, crawled out onto the counter, and reached for the tender. "I can't do it," he gasped.

"Got to," said Mary briefly. "Reach out as far as you can, and I'll sit on your legs."

Bellowing loudly, the calf was drawn on board and deposited in the cabin; bruised and weary, Mr. Williams returned to the deck and reported for orders. "Now what?" he asked.

"Watch those stays," said Mary. "When she jibes, let them go."

"Jesus," said Mr. Williams. "What a night."

"Can you pray?" asked Mary.

"No," said Mr. Williams.

"Well," said Mary, "I guess it don't

matter. There goes the jib. Better haul it in."

Mr. Williams took in the torn jib and stowed it away. The gale was increasing, the wind came after them in sheets, black as rain, tossing the branches, sailing over the earth from great distances, all the air moving and planing, streaming by, steady and full overhead. The *Sarah Pecket* fled along before it, her sail jumping and bellying, ropes whining, tackle rattling; she skittered from one side of the road to the other, she all but rolled her rail under; as each new gust came storming down behind her, she shivered and lay over. If she jibes again, thought Mary, it'll take the mast right out of her. The tiller leaped about in her hand, it took all her strength to hold it; once or twice she found herself on two wheels, and thought she was done. But each time she managed to right herself again, though how she did it, she didn't know. The storm shook the *Sarah Pecket* from stem to stern; it came up behind her like water, blew by and swept ahead; and Mary, at the helm, held her before it, drove her along it, while Mr. Pecket slept in the cabin below, and Mr. Williams knelt on deck, his arms wrapped around the mast. His cheeks were pale, and his lips moved. Oh God, he thought, I hope there's nobody ahead on the road.

And looking back at Mary, he cried out, for comfort:

"How are you, skipper?"

"What?" cried Mary through the boom of the wind.

"Are you all right?"

The words came flying back to her separately, like twigs. She waved to him, and laughed; the wind had blown her hair out like a flag, her eyes were dark with excitement. "I'm all right," she shouted. "Hang on."

And she drew the sail snugger, to round a turn like a clipper, on her beam end.

Mr. Williams hung on. And after a while the terror left him; he found that he could breathe again, he began to feel alive. Down the road they went, rattle and bang, into the darkness ... what a ride; but they were all right so far, they hadn't hit anything yet. That was because Mary was back there at the tiller. Mary wasn't afraid, she knew what she was doing. "I'm all right," she'd said. She was used to boats, she'd been through storms before, she wasn't worried. Well, he thought, she certainly knows how to sail. It was wonderful how the boat stood up to it. He felt almost happy.

"Oh boy," he said; "what a ride."

105

Late that night the *Sarah Pecket* swept like a swallow through the streets of Washington, wind-blown and empty, past the houses of senators and congressmen absent on their vacations. In the wan light of dawn she slipped along beside the Potomac roads littered by the storm.

The wind died, the sun rose; and in its yellow rays Mary cast anchor in the south.

CHAPTER XII

In Which Mr. Pecket Cleans Ship, and Mary Looks at Her Destiny.

The ship lay in the doldrums, becalmed somewhere south of Fredericksburg, in the thirty-eighth latitude. The dusty light of southern noonday beat down upon her decks where Mr. Pecket, on his knees, and in his shirt sleeves, was busy with scrubbing-brush and pail. Now that they were becalmed, he felt that he owed it to Mary to dress ship, polish the bright work, and put his best foot forward.

But something had happened to Mary.

She no longer wanted the *Sarah Pecket* to look like a yacht. "Just so long as we get there," she said to Mr. Pecket, "that's what counts." What had happened was that the storm had made a sailor of her. Nevertheless, she realized that a sailboat, as well as a house, has to be kept clean; and she did not hesitate to do her share of the work.

Now she was feeding the calf from a bottle,

107

and listening to Mr. Williams talk about his youth in the dental college. "It was only a small college," he told her, "not like Harvard or Yale. Still, we had a football team. We used to play the Southern Iowa College of Agriculture and Business Accounting."

"My goodness," said Mary; "did you play football, Henry?"

"No," said Mr. Williams. "I didn't have the time. It was mostly professionals, anyway."

And he added thoughtfully:

"There's a great deal of science in the teeth."

"I'm sure of it," said Mary.

"Yes, sir," said Mr. Williams; "you'd be surprised how much there is to learn."

She looked at him with a sweet but pensive expression. So Mr. Williams was a college man; she hadn't realized that before. Well, yes – you could see there was something different about him; he wasn't at all like the salesmen and clerks she used to wait on at the Hollywood Restaurant. She imagined him seated on the top rail of a fence on the campus, wearing a sweater, and singing *Lehigh Forever*, like Mr. Vallee. How exciting life was, when you had a good look at it.

"Here," she said, "hold the cow a minute, while I pour this milk down his throat."

"Of course," said Mr. Williams modestly, taking hold of the all-too-eager animal, "I never did any sailing before, living so far inland, so to speak. But you ladies here in the east do a lot of it. Miss Whittlesey, now; I've read about her in the papers. And Miss Warbasse. Frostbite sailing, they call it. Why do they call it that, Mary?"

"It's a – a club," said Mary, blushing. She remained silent, struggling with the calf, and trying to remember, in a panic, all she'd ever heard about boats and sailors. "I guess it's in the papers a lot," she said finally, "on account of it's so well known. It's for the ladies," she explained. And she added, going off as fast as she could on another tack:

"I never had any trouble with my teeth. Not to speak of, that is."

At the same time her heart beat because Mr. Williams thought that she was a yachtswoman, like Miss Whittlesey. Well, maybe she was, in a sort of way, if you didn't look too close.

"Everybody has trouble with their teeth," said Mr. Williams, "only they don't bother to find out." And he added politely:

"I'd like to have a look at yours, some time, if you'd like."

Well, thought Mary, my teeth are my own, anyway....

109

"That would be elegant," she said.

But there was still a lot of work to be done on board the *Sarah Pecket*. In the mild, lazy afternoon, they cleaned and oiled the wheels and under-carriage, re-stepped the mast and tightened the stays, and sewed a patch of burlap on the jib. As they worked, Mary and Mr. Williams smiled at each other, and Mr. Pecket hummed to himself a sea-chantey which he had just made up to a tune – if it could be called a tune – of his own. There was something in the air, some half-caught fragrance, some balm and quiet of the south, which made them all feel happy and comfortable. Was it flowers, or history? They did not know. It seemed to them as if there were more space than usual around them; sunny and still the earth spun itself out in deathless peace, in endless summer, already brown, it is true, and stripped of bloom, but never harsh, or lost beneath the ice.

The south... how she lies there, easy and smiling in the sun. It is like coming out of doors again.... In the north the roads lead only to the next town, but here they lead to the world's end – to palms and jungle, river and prairie, to the wilderness in which, perhaps, there are still buffalo and Indians.

That night Mr. Pecket searched the heavens for the Southern Cross. The ship lay still in the motionless air, her lamps shining like a little house at the roadside, red and green to port and starboard, and a riding light at the masthead like a star on a Christmas tree. In the cabin Mary and Mr. Williams talked together in low voices; and Mr. Pecket, seated in the deckhouse, gazed upward at the heavens, in which, however, the Southern Cross was nowhere to be seen. It was a disappointment to him; and it made him feel lonely. His home in the Bronx seemed very far away; he couldn't understand why that didn't please him more. The young people were getting on together, and the boat was doing well, it was all so-far-so-good; but mainly he felt lonesome. Somewhere in the field behind him, the calf, let out to stretch itself at night, gave a plaintive bleat; and the frogs whistled. Those weren't the sounds of home...they were the noises of foreign waters. But where was the Southern Cross? It was funny how it bothered him, not finding what he'd expected.

He thought of Sarah in her bed at home. She had all the familiar things around her...except him. She hadn't found what she was looking for, either.

He shivered a little in the damp night air. There was one thing to be said for Sarah –

you knew what to expect of her. She could raise the devil (she probably had him well raised by now) but there wasn't anything uncertain about life with her. She was careful and saving of her own. Well, he'd chosen to go off, and be uncertain. It was a long, lonely way to southern waters.

The sunny light of morning, fresh and sweet-smelling, woke him to another windless day. His mind was empty, and his body drowsy; he felt happy again, with so much time to himself. It was good to do what he wanted, or nothing at all – to go where he pleased, or to stay where he was, it didn't matter; good to wake up in strange places, along strange roads, where everything was new and pleasant. Since the vessel was still becalmed, he thought he'd do a little caulking, in the event they met with any water. He had no oakum, but he figured rope would do; and instead of pitch or lead, shellac.

He needed no help; and so, while he worked, Mary set herself to have her teeth looked after. She sat on a stone under a tree, leaned back, and opened her mouth as wide as it would go. There's nothing elegant about me now, she thought; but there was no help for it, he couldn't look at her teeth with her mouth shut. She guessed it was all

112

right, one mouth being like another, more or less.

And there was nothing awkward or uncertain about Henry, either, as he bent over her, peering into his little mirror. Seen so close, he looked stern and enormous; and his hands had a clean, soapy smell. He was hurting her lip a little, leaning on it that way. "Ouch," she said, and worked her mouth around to get her lip free.

It was a soft mouth; under his hand it felt like cobwebs. He hadn't expected that, at all. "Hum," he said, and tapped a molar; "does it hurt?"

"No," said Mary.

"There might be a hole in it," he said. He pushed her head back a little. "I want to get the light down into it," he explained.

She lay back among the stones, and closed her eyes. There wasn't very much he could do, except pry and tap; it didn't hurt, and she felt dreamy. It seemed to her that she was in good hands...hands she trusted, deft and strong, young and able, and smelling of soap. A man's hands on her face, closer than ever before, and gentler than she'd expected. A father would be like that...or...or a lover. She opened her eyes dizzily and looked up at him, a wide, dark look, like a child, innocent and beseeching. The sun was behind him, his fresh young face, so serious, so intent, was in shadow; his eyes looked back at her like an owl, seeing her, seeing deep into her eyes....

When is the moment of falling in love? How deep must the look go, before the answering look rises to meet it, swept upward from the heart like a bird or a current? Which is the moment of seeing, when what was known before turns strange, and what was strange is strange no longer, but recalled as though from a dream. What sudden glance or silence, what lifted hand or piteous look, fragrance, light upon flesh, unspoken promise, knocks on the door of memory, lights the warm lamp of seeing, opens to hunger again, to the Thou-art-mine of the spirit, the I-am-thine of the heart? No one can say; there is no rule, there is no history. It comes in silence; the moment is full of doubt and wonder.

Mary said nothing; and Mr. Williams said nothing. They looked at each other, unable to look away...feeling the world changing, the tide rising, the mist descending. Then Mary spoke, faintly, and in a dream. "Thank you," she said.

"Don't mention it," said Mr. Williams. And he turned away, back to the ship.

The spell was broken; but the arrow was

sped, the wound was mortal. And all that day Mary's heart sat trembling in her breast; and Mr. Williams's breath kept failing him. Only Mr. Pecket went on with his caulking, unaware; he thought the south had gotten into their bones.

That night a fog hid the stars; gray and cold it hung like moss from the trees, and from the spreader of the *Sarah Pecket,* whose lights shone dimly in the mist, each with a little ring around it like the moon. Everything was still, the fields on either side were lost in silence, the fog muffled all. Mr. Williams sat on deck to keep his watch, and Mary sat with him, wrapped in Mr. Pecket's coat. They said nothing; they, too, were cold and still, like the trees.

"Henry," said Mary at last. She put out her hand; shy and unsure, it lay curled near him like a little leaf, he could take it or not.... He took it in his own, it trembled with cold. "Mary," he said.

"Yes," she whispered.

"I don't know," he said. And they stared out at the fog together, with beating hearts.

"Don't you, Henry?" she asked at last. "I do... I think."

"Maybe I do, too," he said. She tightened her fingers around his. "It's queer," she said, "isn't it? I mean... you and me...."

"Is it?" he asked. The fog was in his throat; he could do no more than croak. "Is it . . . Mary?"

"Isn't it?" she asked, lifting her face to his. He stared at her; she looked as white and wavery as the mist.

"Maybe it is," he said; and sighing, leaned and kissed her.

Her nose was cold; and her face was soft as snow. He hadn't looked for anything so mortal. . . . He put his arm around her and drew her close. "Do you?" he asked.

"Yes," she said, "I guess I do."

She leaned her face against his shoulder. What had she said? And what had he? Nothing . . . or everything . . . she didn't know. Her heart was as still as the fields around her; as for the future, she didn't think about it at all . . . her hopes, her dreams, the boudoir of glass and silver, the ermine coat . . . gone from her mind like the past, like being poor and lonely, like waiting for Mr. Right . . . gone, gone. . . .

Mr. Williams also let his thoughts lie quiet, without asking them what he should do. Who was she? He didn't know; rich or poor, high or low, he'd never stopped to ask. She took his finger, and kissed it. "Don't do that," he said; and drew in his breath. He smelled the simple fragrance of her hair, he

116

felt her face against his hand, cold and tender. How fragile she was, how like a dream the fog, the slow fumble of his heart; it was too much, it was too much to bear....

"Oh," he cried, overcome by what had happened to him, humbled and unworthy, "so do I!"

CHAPTER XIII

In Which Mr. Schultz Fouls His Rudder on the Law.

But in the morning, in the clear light of day, he was full of fears: he remembered hearing about poor men who had fallen in love with wealthy girls, and nothing good had come of it, either. Was she rich? Look at the way she handled a boat, as though she were born to it. Suppose she was only playing with him? That was what rich girls did. Or suppose she was serious, and wanted to marry him; had he ought to? Thoroughly confused, and in a crafty manner, he approached Mr. Pecket, to see what he could find out about her.

"I suppose," he said, "you couldn't give me an idea of where you're aiming for?"

In this way he hoped to discover what sort of home was waiting for her at the end of the voyage.

Mr. Pecket was seated by the roadside with his charts, which consisted of U.S.

Geodetic Survey No. 1222, and some road maps of Louisa and Hanover counties, given out by the Standard Oil Company of Virginia. "If the wind picks up," he said, "we'll be at Beaver Dam before nightfall." He wet his finger in his mouth, and held it up. "West by nor'west," he declared; "it has a healthy feel to it. Get your sails up, Mr. Williams; all three of them."

"Hadn't we better start rolling first?" asked Mr. Williams. "It goes easier that way."

"That don't signify," said Mr. Pecket. "It may be easier, but it's less seamanlike. Never let go your mooring till you've got your wind, Mr. Williams. That'll keep you off the rocks."

Mr. Williams went thoughtfully back to the ship, and upped sail. Mary helped him cleat down the halyard while he hauled at the throat. As she passed him, on her way to set the jib, she gave him a shy and shining glance. "Do you?" she whispered.

He nodded, mute and uneasy. Don't let go your mooring, he thought, till you've got the wind.

And he imagined himself drifting upon the rocks of society, amid the general scorn.

Mr. Pecket climbed on board, and the ship moved off, not without several good shoves

119

from Mr. Williams. And Mary leaned out over the stern, to say good-by to the calf, who followed in the dinghy. Good-by, she thought, little cow; I hope you'll be as happy as I am. Things have changed for both of us, for you and me both. It isn't what I looked for, but it doesn't matter ... even if he's poor, it's being in love that counts. We'll have a little house somewhere in the country where people can come to have their teeth fixed. Maybe I'll see you again some day, when you're big. Only I won't know it's you, I guess.

She looked over her shoulder at Mr. Williams, who was standing in the fo'c'sle; only his head showed above the forward scuttle, gazing gloomily forward, toward Beaver Dam and Richmond. And all at once her heart turned over with anxiety. He looked so stern, there, from the rear – what she could see of him, that is. I wonder, she thought, if he knows about me. I wonder if he knows I was a waitress in a restaurant.

I don't have to tell him, she decided; there's no law. Nothing can make me.

And squatting down next to Mr. Pecket, she whispered:

"Tell me something about yachting."

However, all Mr. Pecket was able to tell her had to do with excursions in Arctic waters or in the Indian Ocean, bits of nautical fancy which were of no help to her whatever.

The wind blew fresh and fair, west nor'west as Mr. Pecket had said, and the *Sarah Pecket* ran gayly over the level, red-dirt roads to Beaver Dam. There, at evening, she drew up before the butcher shop of Mr. Ralph Menaby – a sight which caused Mary to turn pale, bite her lip, and finally burst into tears. "He didn't say his cousin was a butcher," she cried. "Don't let him have it.

"Oh, my poor dear little calf."

"That would be stealing," said Mr. Pecket; and Mr. Williams, whose two dollars were at stake, agreed with him. Mary was led below, tearful and protesting; the calf was handed over to his destiny; and, with money in his pocket, Mr. Williams invited his shipmates to dinner. "What I think of, mostly," he declared, "is a stew, with onions."

At these words, Mary wept anew. "Go away," she cried.

And she added, between her sobs,

"I'll never eat again."

Nor could their combined coaxing and wheedling so much as cause her to lift her tear-stained face from the pillow.

So Mr. Pecket and Mr. Williams had their

stew by themselves. Then, feeling full, warm, and happy, Mr. Pecket went off to send a postal home to his wife. It was a foolish thing to do, perhaps; at any other time he might have hesitated. But he kept thinking he'd told Mary he would; and that he owed her something for the calf. And then, besides, he'd made a turn, and doubled his money – or, anyhow, Mr. Williams's money – and in a vague sort of way he wanted Sarah to know about it.

He was a long time choosing the right card. Finally he picked out a picture of a garden full of flowers; and writing on it:

Greetings from Valparaiso,

dropped it in the box at the post office.

At least she wouldn't know where he was. And comforted in that assurance, he turned in, and went to sleep.

Alas for the hopes with which men never fail to delude themselves. Two days later Mrs. Pecket, in the Bronx, received a postcard, on which was written, in her husband's hand:

Greetings from Valparaiso.

But on the bottom of the card were printed the words:

Greetings from Beaver Dam, Virginia.

Mrs. Pecket gave herself a day to think it over. Then she tore up the postal, and went

122

to see Mr. Schultz. "Well," she said, "I've found him, the old fool."

"So," said Mr. Schultz. "Where is he?"

"Never mind," said Mrs. Pecket. "I'm going after him myself." And she gave Mr. Schultz a gloomy look, as though to say: If there's going to be any trouble made for him, I'm the one who is going to make it.

Returning to her house, she packed her bag, and counted up her money. She took her time; her motions were unhurried, but firm. She had missed Mr. Pecket, not so much out of tenderness as from a sense of possession; he was her capital, with which she did the works of her spirit. These works were dear to her, because there was nothing easy about them. They were works of survival in a hostile world. To live at all was hard, but it excited her; it did not frighten her, she did not want to run away. Nevertheless she felt that she had been betrayed; and that her good plans had been brought to nothing. She had done a bit of business, to put food in her mouth, and clothes on her back; and she had had it taken out from under her nose by an old man who didn't care where his next meal was coming from. She meant to have him back again – by the ear, if necessary; to say nothing of the *Sarah Pecket,* which belonged by right to Mr. Schultz, and not to her husband at all.

Mr. Schultz, on his side, had no doubt about his rights, although the lawyer to whom he had gone for advice confessed himself puzzled. There were a great many questions involved, including the matter of just when Mr. Schultz might have been said to have taken possession. In addition, there was the question of jurisdiction. "As I see it," he told the butcher, "it's like this: A buys a boat from B. Very good; that's all plain sailing; and we have, to begin with, a case for the court of original jurisdiction, which, in this instance, is the Supreme Court of the State of New York. The money is paid; but has title been transferred? That is a point for the court to decide. Very well, then: before the petitioner can enjoy the fruits of his purchase, C steals the boat, or at least disappears with it, causing A to lose the comfort, pleasure, convenience, and also the income from said boat. Am I right? Very good. So it's all at once a case of piracy, and they move us into the court of admiralty. But –" and here he looked distressed – "piracy, to be piracy proper, must be committed on the high seas, or at least upon inland waters, as in the case or cases of pirates operating on the Yangtze-kiang

124

River. Well, there you see the problem; can the Bronx be so considered? I am inclined to doubt it. Nevertheless, I am afraid that if we move in the court of original jurisdiction, we shall be directed to bring suit in the court of admiralty. Or vice versa."

"All right," said Mr. Schultz impatiently, "bring suit in any court you please. Stealing is stealing, meat or boats. So don't bother me with hair-splitting, but get my lunch-counter back."

"Ah," said the lawyer, "a lunch-counter. Well, you see . . . that makes a different case of it again. I thought you said it was a boat."

Mr. Schultz returned to his butcher shop, where a chop was a chop, and a roast was a roast. The next day he went over to see Mrs. Pecket; he meant to tell her a few things. But Mrs. Pecket was gone; she had left for the south, by overland bus.

CHAPTER XIV

Mr. Pecket Goes Fishing.

To Mr. Pecket, sailing in the balmy weather off Ashland, there was no question about the *Sarah Pecket* being a boat. He knew what she was by the feeling of joy with which he watched the sails fill out and draw, and the pleasure and bustle of getting under weigh each morning, and, pushed by Mr. Williams, leaving his moorings astern. The sun burned his face; the wind wafted him onward; and his thoughts no longer concerned themselves with the land.

It was near the Pomunkey River that he first decided to go fishing. However, he did not intend to do the usual sort of fishing, with a hook and sinker. What he had in mind was something more exciting; swordfishing, or even whaling. But first of all there were some changes to make in the *Sarah Pecket;* and he cast anchor for this purpose.

With Mr. Williams to help him, he set about building a fisherman's pulpit, and a
126

mast-head look-out. Both pulpit and look-out were small, owing to the lack of materials; he was obliged to use the floorboards of the fo'c'sle, the anchor rope, and the jib halyard. He expected to dispense with the jib altogether, in order to have more room in which to flourish his harpoon. The question of how to reach the look-out, he left to Mary; being so much the smallest, there was no use her expecting anybody else to do it.

When he told her that he wanted her to climb half way up the mast and sit there, she uttered a cry of indignation. "Never," she exclaimed. "I'm no bird."

"We'll push you up," said Mr. Pecket hopefully. "You'll have a lovely view."

"No," said Mary.

"Why not?" asked Mr. Pecket.

"I don't want to," said Mary. "Besides," she added firmly, "I'd look silly up there."

"Not in southern waters, you wouldn't," said Mr. Pecket. And he went on to explain:

"All the boats go fishing in the south. It's what they mostly do."

He wanted the *Sarah Pecket* to be like every other boat. But Mary was frightened. "I won't do it," she cried. "You can't make me." But a moment later she thought of Mr. Williams, and how she was supposed to be a member of the Frostbite Club. Oh misery, she thought; what would he think of her if she refused? Perhaps real lady sailors were used to climbing masts, and sitting down on little bits of wood high up in the air... how could she tell? And what ever did he think of her, anyway? She wished she knew. He'd been so silent and anxious ever since that night... if she was, really, what she'd let him think, wouldn't she just naturally climb up there and sit down like she was used to it?

"Well," she said faintly, "all right... only... is it high enough? I mean... will I see anything?"

"Can't get it any higher," said Mr. Pecket. "It'll do, I guess, things being sort of close underfoot, anyhow."

With the platform rigged to the mast, and the pulpit bolted to the forward deck, there was only the harpoon left to deal with. This Mr. Pecket put together from the spinnaker pole and the kitchen knife. Then he announced himself ready. "Up you go," he said to Mary; and up she went, with all hands heaving at her bottom.

Eight feet in the air, dizzy and out of breath, she eased herself down on the little platform, and looked around. Her shins hurt, and she'd scraped her elbow; she felt giddy, it seemed like a mile high. She looked down at the deck, and all but fell off again. "All right," she said, gritting her teeth; "get going."

But to herself she prayed: "O god, let me act like a lady."

They hoisted sail behind her; Mr. Pecket climbed out onto the pulpit, Mr. Williams got behind and pushed; and Mary closed her eyes and clutched the mast. When she opened them again, they were sailing.

She took a breath, and looked around. It was like being in a tree; she could see the country, wide and brown around her, misty in the sun. It was lovely country, it looked friendly, it had a sweet, airy smell to it. And it wasn't bad, being up there on the mast, once she got used to it; it rocked a little, and going round corners bothered her, she seemed to fly off into space; but the road was fairly straight. ... She looked up at the clouds, so white and clean and lovely; they seemed more at home there in the south than they used to, up north. They had always seemed to be going somewhere, passing over, not liking it, or wanting to stay; this must be where they'd been going. This drowsy, friendly land.... It must be nice to be at home in the world, as light and easy as a cloud. She'd never thought very much about being at home anywhere in particular; it had always been more of a question what she'd have in the way of furniture when she got there. But she could see now – though only dimly, still – that it wasn't furniture she wanted most, but feeling that she belonged somewhere, comfortable, a part of earth... the earth strong and good beneath her, the air smelling sweet all around.... There she was, half way up a mast, with no more to her name than what she had on her back, or stowed away in her locker; and feeling more at home than she'd ever felt in her life. As long as she didn't go round corners, that is. It was strangely comforting; though upsetting, too, in a way, because what had happened to her ideals? She couldn't very well better herself by climbing masts...or could she? And Mr. Williams...what of him? He was a dentist, and not a success; not a banker, or a district attorney. Still, she was happy; and that was what counted.

What did he think of her, sitting up there in the air as though she were used to it? Nothing but good, she hoped; she hoped he was glad she was brave.

Well...where were the swordfish; and what was she to do?

"Ahoy, up there," called Mr. Pecket anxiously. "Don't you see anything?"

"Not so's I'd notice," she answered.

"Well, take a good look," he told her.

He stood at the bow, the harpoon in his hand, peering out at what he saw. It was all blue water to him, the long swells, and the salt sea-air. At the same time, he was prepared for accidents on land. "Hard to port, Mr. Williams," he cried. "Keep her out of the ditch.

"You, Kelly . . . do you see anything?"

She waved to him gayly. "There's a chicken coming through the hedge," she said. "Don't run over it."

"Where?" asked Mr. Pecket.

"Dead ahead," said Mary.

Mr. Pecket leaned eagerly out over the pulpit. "A little to port, Mr. Williams," he called. "Ease your sheet. Steady does it." And he balanced the harpoon in his hand.

"Look out," said Mary; "you're going to hit it." She leaned forward, in sudden fear. "Hey," she cried; "what are you doing?"

Mr. Pecket did not reply. Instead, he stretched as far out as he could, as though to urge the vessel on, and brandished the spinnaker pole. The chicken, skittering through the hedge, stood still for a moment; then turned, with a cluck, and started down the road. The *Sarah Pecket* came on at good speed; the chicken ran ahead, faster and faster as the ship gained on it, no longer

131

silent, but squawking away for dear life. The bow of the vessel rose up behind its back, with Mr. Pecket leaning far out, like a figurehead. Up on the mast, Mary gave a shriek. "Don't do it," she cried.

"Starboard your helm, Mr. Williams," bellowed Mr. Pecket.

"No," cried Mary. "Oh, poor little chicken."

Wrapping her arms around the mast, she shut her eyes. "Oh dear," she whispered. "Oh my." Far down below, the chicken ran from side to side, squawking and fluttering, but never off the road; like a flying fish or a dolphin it skipped along in front of the boat in a foam of feathers. "Steady all," muttered Mr. Pecket.

And with a cry, he hurled the harpoon.

The knife missed; but the pole gave the bird a rap in passing, and the rope tangled in its legs. It turned head over heels; then, squawking even louder than before, started for the side of the road.

"Loose the dinghy, Mr. Williams," ordered Mr. Pecket. "We'll have to go after it."

Mr. Williams put on his brakes, and let the sail go free; the *Sarah Pecket* came to a stop, and Mr. Pecket climbed into the tender. "Got to do this thing right," he explained.

But when he came around the boat's side to where the chicken had been, there was a farmer waiting for him, with a pitchfork. "What all's been goin' on here?" he wanted to know.

Mr. Pecket looked at the man in surprise. Then slowly, and with an air of wonder, he glanced around him, up and down – at the brown fields, and the hedge, the road, the distant trees. There was no water . . . no water anywhere. There was no sea, no blue and rolling swell . . . where had it all gone? And then, at last, it occurred to him that perhaps he had not been fishing for swordfish, after all. He grew pale; and his hands trembled. "Well," he said, "it's my mistake, mister."

"So it is," said the farmer sourly. "But you can make it good in jail, I reckon."

"In jail?" echoed Mr. Pecket faintly.

"That's what I said," declared the man. "I guess you heard me. It's lucky you're white folks; if you were black, I'd stick this fork into you right here and now. Chicken-stealing. You come along with me."

With the harpoon in one hand, the pitchfork in the other, he prodded Mr. Pecket away from the boat, and into the middle of the road. "We're going down to Ashland together," he said, "you and me. There's a sheriff there'll take care of you.

Yes, sir; this world is full of poison. It takes a man all his time to keep it straight."

And with the sharp prongs of the fork within an inch of his behind, Cap'n Hector Pecket of the sloop *Sarah Pecket* of New York stepped off down the road to Ashland and the county jail.

CHAPTER XV

And Lands Mary's Fish for Her.

"I don't know what's the matter with people, they're so mean," said Mary. "Oh, Henry." Her eyes filled with tears, and she clung to Mr. Williams's arm. "They'd ought to know he wasn't stealing," she said.

The two of them had just come from the courthouse, where they had heard the judge sentence Mr. Pecket to pay a fine of twenty-five dollars or spend a month in jail. Now they stood together on the street outside, and counted their money. "I've got four dollars," said Mr. Williams, "and a little over. What have you got?"

"Three," said Mary. "And Mr. Pecket has less than me."

"That makes about ten," said Mr. Williams, "and we've got to have some left over to eat. Is three dollars really all you've got, Mary?"

She blushed, and turned away. Well, she thought, it's come; now he knows. There's

135

no use pretending any more. "Yes," she said; "that's all."

"Well, then," said Mr. Williams, "we're here for the winter."

Slowly, without saying anything, they walked back through the little town to the ship, which they had left moored to an old fence by the roadside. The *Sarah Pecket* looked lonely and forlorn; and Mr. Williams and Mary also were forlorn, and silent. They held each other's hand, and sighed. A month in jail . . . it was a long, long time. What ever would they do?

They sat down together on the deck and let their legs hang over the side. The slow sweet southern evening came down around them, the twilight deepened; in the town a few lights were lit, a car went by on the road. And still they sat, silent and anxious, tasting the cool and fragrant air, lonely for Mr. Pecket and for each other . . . lonely for what they'd come to love, the evening bustle of the ship, with the sail slacking, and the anchor ready to be heaved over, for the sail coming down, and the sound of halyards running out, and tackle creaking, for the quiet and peace of evening at a mooring. . . . How often had it been like that. And now the cold hand of the law had stopped them, had frozen them solid, halfway to nowhere. What were they going to do, with only seven dollars between them? They couldn't make believe any longer – not without Mr. Pecket; he'd been the one who had held it all together and made it seem real. Maybe I can get some teeth to fill, thought Mr. Williams, or some scissors to sharpen. Only seven dollars, and Mary has three; she ought to send home for more. But all at once he thought: Perhaps she hasn't any more; and his heart beat with mystery and doubt. And Mary, in the dusk, in which the dew was already falling, thought of Mr. Pecket all alone by himself in jail, no more a sailor, no longer free to come and go . . . poor Mr. Pecket, he'd always hated to be meddled with.

"We'd better set our riding lights," she said at last. "He'd have wanted us to."

Mr. Williams lighted the lamps; then he came and stood uneasily at her side. "I guess I'll turn in," he said.

"Yes," she agreed, "we might as well. There's milk in the galley if you want it, and some bread."

"I'm not hungry," he said. "Goodnight, Mary."

"Goodnight, Henry." She turned her face away; she could see that he wasn't going to kiss her. Well, she didn't want him to, as a matter of fact.

He went forward to the fo'c'sle and lay down. And Mary curled herself up in the cockpit, with her coat over her. The frogs sang, at the edge of town; and the moon in the west made the sky look light. She closed her eyes. Where was the sweetness now? I've been making believe I was happy, she thought, and all the time I'd only three dollars left. Now he knows I'm not rich, or a lady, and it's all over and finished with. She thought of the past, of her little room in the north, so neat and dry and lonely; how far away from it she was, and no way to get back to it, perhaps ever. She thought of the flight across the bridge in the storm, the days which followed, the white sails in the sun, the clouds overhead, the sweet fresh wind . . . the little calf. . . . It was worth it, she said; and wept, for the little calf, and for herself, and for the good times that were over and that would never be the same again. They hadn't lasted very long. . . .

That night she slept fitfully, curled in the cockpit, under the wagon-tongue. But she knew what she had to do. Early the next morning, before Mr. Williams was up, she hurried into town, to look for work. But it was noon before she found it, at the Old South Tea Room and Cafeteria: eight dollars a week, and tips, if there were any – to wait on table, dry dishes, and give a hand with the cooking. At that, she was lucky; they'd had a girl, right there from Ashland, a town girl, but she'd up and married a man from West Virginia. It was the only job in town; she wouldn't have got it at all, for they'd rather have had a town girl who knew the customers, if it hadn't been for her coming from the north, and having experience in the big restaurants up there; it gave the Old South a tone, to have a foreigner working in the kitchen.

Mary put on the apron they gave her, and the cap. In two weeks, she thought, she'd have made enough – with what they had – to get Mr. Pecket out of jail. Otherwise, she'd almost rather die than what she was doing, it was so much like what she had run away from. If only Mr. Williams didn't come in and see her there; that would be the last misery. Well, she owed the skipper that, too, she guessed; he'd shared what he had with her. Maybe Henry would find somewheres else to eat.

But Henry came into the Old South Tea Room and Cafeteria that very same day, to get his lunch. He'd been going up and down town with his cart with the grindstone in it, and the sign which said: *Teeth Filled. Knives and Scissors Ground;* but he hadn't found anything to do. He was hungry, and tired; he left his cart outside, by the curb, and sat down at a table where he could watch it. Mary crept up behind him, and gave him the bill-of-fare over his shoulder. "Hello, Henry," she said, with what felt like a fishbone in her throat.

He turned around and looked at her in her cap and apron; and his eyes widened. "Hello," he said finally. "I wondered where you were."

"Well," she said faintly, "I'm here."

"I see," he said. He looked down at his hands, spread out on the table-cloth. "I guess I'm not hungry," he said, and pushed back his chair. Then, without another word, he got up and went out. Her mouth trembled as she turned back to the kitchen. Well, she told him in her mind, I can't help it, can I, if this is all I am? I never said I was anything else; if you thought so, that was your fault.

But her heart, as she dried the dishes that afternoon, was heavy as lead. You might have been a little nicer to me, she told him; you might have said you didn't care. You might have said you liked me anyhow, no matter what I was.

That night she went back to the boat with slow, unwilling steps. It wouldn't have surprised her to find it dark and deserted, and Mr. Williams gone too, like the rest of the good times. But he was waiting for her; he helped her in over the side. "Hello, Mary," he said. It was queer, she thought, he didn't sound angry at all.

She sat down wearily in the cockpit. "I'm tired, Henry," she told him. "My feet hurt me."

He sat down next to her, and put his coat around her shoulders. It was chilly there, in the evening. "Why did you do it, Mary?" he asked. "We had enough to live on, here on the boat. You didn't need to do that. It makes me feel bad."

She laid her hand on his arm, in a gesture at once timid and grateful. "Thanks, Henry," she said, "that's nice of you. I was afraid you were mad at me. But we can't let Mr. Pecket stay in jail. We've got to get him out."

"I know," he said. "But still... it's hard on you, Mary."

"I'm used to it," she said.

He looked at her, and then he looked away. "Is that what you were, up home?" he asked in a low voice. "A waitress?"

"Yes," she answered. ...
"That's what I was."

"Why didn't you tell me?" he said.

"You didn't ask me," she answered. "You
141

thought I was something else. Well . . . so did I, too, almost, for a while.

"I sort of thought you wanted me to be."

And as he made no reply, she added:

"So you know, now. I'm sorry, Henry; maybe I shouldn't have let you think things that weren't true. I guess you won't like me any more. I don't know as I blame you."

He took her hand in his, cold and small as a little stone. "That isn't true," he said. "I like you more this way, Mary. I was worried about the other."

"You don't have to say that," she told him. "I'm all right. I know you didn't mean anything . . . that night on deck."

"No," he said, "you're wrong. I did mean it . . . only I got scared." And he told her what he'd been afraid of, how he'd seen himself being made a fool. "I thought you were maybe just playing with me," he said.

"I guess maybe I was," said Mary. She lay back in his arms, suddenly weary, suddenly at peace, her knees gone weak, her heart flooded with comfort. "But not like what you thought."

"No," he said gently, "not like what I thought." He laid his face down against her cheek. "Oh Mary," he said, "do you . . . still?"

Speechless, she rubbed her cheek against

142

his. "We'll be poor," he told her, "for a long time yet."

"I'm glad of that," she said. "Just so long as you like me."

CHAPTER XVI

Mr. Pecket's Flood.

Mr. Pecket lay on his cot in the jail. Through the small window high in the wall he could see the sky, and clouds going by like sails, free and airy. He, too, had been free – free to drift like a cloud or a sail across the land and the water, to breathe the air of foreign places, to see new sights, and warm his nose in the sun. But that was all over, that was in the past. The cloudy skippers ran up their skyey tops'ls, and turned in the breeze along the tides of air; they looked down upon earth, and set their courses by the stars and winds. No more for him, not till a month was up, not till after he'd been dried out like an old bone, lying there in the shadow, kept away from sun and wind; and the *Sarah Pecket* rotted by the roadside and grew fungus on her bottom.

He wondered where she was, and whether Mr. Williams had moored her safely; maybe Mary had taken over, she was the better sailor of the two. She was a good girl, Mary; but what would she do now? He wondered was she waiting for him, or had she gone ahead, south, where she was bound. When he thought of not finding her there when he got out, his spirits sank even lower than before. But it was unlikely that she'd wait; she had her own life to live. It was queer; he'd been with a woman all this time, and he'd never even thought about it. He'd been wilder than he knew, and never given it a thought.

He missed her; but he was glad she couldn't see him lying there in jail. It took his pride away, it made him feel the way he used to. Would he ever see her again, he wondered. And Mr. Williams...what would the dentist do now? Push his cart along the roads again, he guessed. They'd been happy together, the three of them, they'd got along well together, sailing here and sailing there.... It had been a wonderful voyage, but it was over. The voyage was ended.

They had their lives to live, Mary and Mr. Williams; they owed him nothing. But now they were on their way south – or west. What else could they do?

He shook his head and groaned. What a muddle he'd made of things, from beginning to end. And how he'd meddled with others

– for all his talk of leaving others be. What had come over him? All he'd wanted was to be left alone. And he'd taken a boat that wasn't his to take; he'd cheated the government of a calf, he'd changed the course of a young girl's life, he'd all but killed a chicken; what an old fool he was. He'd done everything he didn't want others to do; and relished it, besides. Wherever he'd stepped, he'd trod on someone's toes.

It frightened him to be locked up. It was like being dead; so many things were happening outside, and he couldn't see them: the earth going on about its business, from sunrise to sunset, through the morning colors, the deep noonday tide, the clouds of evening...things going on, just as he'd been going on across the earth, before they'd stopped him, made him take his sails down, and fold up his charts. He'd been without a care, almost – but now that he couldn't move any more, he was frightened. Suppose it all caught up with him again – the dry, the lonely past. And death – death was there, too, waiting for him some day – to roll him up in stillness like in a jail. There wasn't even love, to help him over that hour....

The old thought of a flood returned to him: a flood to wash the earth clean again.

Only this time it seemed as if the rising waters were meant for him.

And there he was, caught like a rat in a trap. . . .

Terror seized him; he wanted to get back to his boat again. There he'd be safe. He sprang to his feet and threw himself at the bars of his cell. "Let me out of here," he cried. "Let me go. There's something awful going to happen."

But no one answered; only a Negro, in the next cell, murmured sadly: "Hallelujah."

Overcome with mortification, weak and dejected, Mr. Pecket sank down on his cot, and closed his eyes. There was nothing to be done; he must wait. Perhaps, when the month was up, he'd find his boat again. Perhaps the flood would wait, too.

But during the night the clouds came up; and while he slept, shivering and uneasy, the last storm of autumn broke over the south. When he awoke, the world was gray and damp, and he gazed in horror at the sky from which the long, slanting lines of rain descended with a mournful sound, blown by the wind.

Yet at that moment his troubles were nearly over. Rescue was at hand, though not what he expected. Towards evening the door of his cell was opened, and he was set free.

147

Thankful and bewildered, he stepped across the threshold into the arms of his wife Sarah, who did not, however, embrace him.

"*Valparaiso,*" was all she said.

And she folded her arms in an angry manner.

She had followed him down from Beaver Dam. In that moment he saw himself trapped; he saw his ship a lunch-counter, and he saw his travels over...escape cut off, the walls rising about him, shut away for the rest of his life from the world of cloud and wind, of mist and mooring, from the Bay of Fundy and the Caribbean...an old hulk in the grass of his yard, a buried keel in the snow. One prison or another; what was the difference? With a muffled cry, he sprang forward, and shaking off the hands which strove to hold him, fled past her, out of the jail, into the rain.

He ran; the rain drenched him, water dripped from his face and trickled down his neck, his feet spattered in the mud, his trousers clung to his knees. Past the motion-picture palace he ran, past the five-and ten-cent store, the lighted windows of the Old South, the post office, the garage and livery stable; past the cottage in which Mr. Williams was sharpening someone's pruning shears.... His breath was failing him, he had a pain in his side, and his legs ached; but he kept going. They mustn't get me, he thought; they mustn't get me ever again. Far up the road stood the *Sarah Pecket,* moored to the fence, empty and dark. With a sob of relief, he saw the familiar outlines before him; drenched and exhausted, he dragged himself over the side; with trembling fingers he unloosed the mooring rope, ran up the sail, and pushed off. The wind caught her, she swayed, tipped, creaked all over, and started . . . slowly, gathering speed, her nose to the east, to where the wind-blown waters of the Pomunkey, swollen by the rain, moved in leaden ripples to the sea.

Once more he held the helm; once more the sheet tautened at his side, the sail loomed and sang in the dark. It was like the night on the bridge; the rain pelted at his back, the wind whistled behind him; and he felt a wild and somber joy. They hadn't got him; he was still skipper of his ship, free to sail, from north to south, from west to east. The night was foggy black, he couldn't see ahead . . . no matter, the seas were wide, the ship would hold. Solid timber, stout hull, brave sails. . . . A branch whipped his face, he struck at it in the darkness. "Go on," he cried, "go on."

Escape – that was it: escape from what he'd done, from what he'd been, from all the

149

fears and doubts which made up his little world. He wondered how his wife had found him; but it didn't matter, since she had. He remembered her look as she stood there in the doorway, and his heart failed him. How she must hate me, he thought, to look at me like that. "Faster," he cried to the wind, "faster." He had to get on; he had to put the sea behind him, before she caught up to him, before she took him back with her again, to the city, to the Schneiders and the Schultzes, to the shelves that didn't fit, to the little plot of ground in the Bronx – to a world without love or joy, from which he would never escape again. . . .

The road was empty, rain-swept and wind-swept; the water hissed from his wheels like spray. Behind him, far off toward Ashland, a headlight gleamed pale and silver-yellow in the rain; and then another. They were coming after him. No matter, they'd never catch him . . . not any more. He thought he must be somewhere near the sea. It was time. "Kelly," he called to the empty dark, "set up the jib." He clutched the wagon-tongue tighter, with both hands. "Ready about," he cried; and "hard-alee." The ship lurched and settled, the sail slackened and caught again with a crack. He threw his weight against the helm. The nose of the

Sarah Pecket swept in a circle, the wheels ran up over the road's edge, skittered in the mud, ran on . . . the deck sloped downward. Below her lay the river.

She went into it with a crash; the water jumped, then rose and smothered her. She never floated; she just settled down, as wet inside as out. The mast snapped as her bottom hit the water, and the sail folded over like a broken wing. Mr. Pecket gave one cry: "Sarah"; and that was all. Behind him, on the road, the two cars drew up with a screech of brakes; doors were flung open, and forms hurried out and galloped down the bank after him. "Hector," they cried; and "Skipper."

They drew him out, Mary and Mr. Williams, while Mrs. Pecket and the sheriff watched from the river's edge. He was pale, and his eyes were closed; he was all but drowned. They shook him and kneaded him, pumped his arms, and spilled some water out. Then they bundled him up in a blanket and took him back to the jail. It was the only place they could find for him, that time of night.

He sat up on his cot, shivering and weak, while they fed him hot soup and whisky. A little color came back into his cheeks, and he sighed. "Well," he said, "she didn't float, did she?"

He looked at Mary and Mr. Williams; and they looked back at him with gentle smiles. "I thought you'd gone," he said. "I thought you'd left me."

His gaze travelled from their faces, shining with happiness and love, to their fingers twined about each other. "So," he said slowly, nodding his head. "Well, that's good. I didn't think of it.

"But it's all over now; I can't do any more."

And then, to his surprise, instead of scolding him, Mrs. Pecket bent over and kissed him. "You old fool," she said. "You can come home, can't you?"

"Well, I don't know," said Mr. Pecket. He put his hand out and touched her cheek; it was wet, and not from rain, either. "Why," he said, "you're crying."

"What if I am?" demanded Mrs. Pecket fiercely.

He lay back again, and closed his eyes. It was all too much for him; and he gave a long, wondering sigh. "Well," he said –

"Home..."

"Yes," he said; "I guess I can."